W.i.t.c.h.

Will   Irma   Taranee   Cornelia   Hay Lin

Keeping Hope

Adapted by **KATE EGAN**

This book was first published in the USA in 2004 by Volo/Hyperion Books for Children
First published in Great Britain in 2007 by HarperCollins *Children's Books*, a division of
HarperCollins Publishers Ltd.

© 2007 Disney Enterprises, Inc.

ISBN13: 978-0-00-722220-9
ISBN10: 0-00-722220-3

1 3 5 7 9 10 8 6 4 2

The HarperCollins website is:
www.harpercollinschildrensbooks.co.uk

Visit www.clubwitch.co.uk

Printed and bound in Italy

ONE

Butterflies fluttered in Hay Lin's stomach as she got ready to launch into her What-I-Did-on-My-Summer-Vacation story. She'd heard all of the words she was about to say fly out of her friends' mouths before: boys; crushes; dates. But she'd always been the audience when they came up . . . never the one who was front and centre and saying the lines. Suddenly she was developing a major case of stage fright!

It was nice to be in the limelight for once, Hay Lin had to admit. But somehow it doesn't feel like me! she thought. She still couldn't believe all that had happened since her friends had left town and summer vacation had come and gone. She couldn't wait to spill the details – but she was a little worried about what her friends would think . . . or say.

Hay Lin took a deep breath and looked at them. Will, Irma, Cornelia, and Taranee were all gazing at her with full attention, waiting for her to begin.

Here are the four people I want to hang out with most in the whole world, Hay Lin told herself. Well, four of the five, anyway. Maybe I'll see the other one later. He might even be in one of my classes! I can trust them. And, no matter what they think of my story, there's one major side benefit of telling it. I get to relive every moment of meeting my first major crush! I get to say his name out loud! Hay Lin tried not to giggle.

And so she began to tell her friends the whole story. . . .

It had all started when Hay Lin was in Heatherfield Park, Rollerblading all by herself . . . which was something she did all the time. Usually she was really great at Rollerblading, but that day there seemed to be something wrong with her. She was totally off balance! She couldn't remember what she was thinking, but for some reason she'd decided to get an ice-cream cone, even though she was having a hard time staying up as she skated.

As soon as she held the cone, Hay Lin knew she'd made a mistake. She decided to skate over to a bench and eat the ice cream sitting down. But she was so focused on not dropping the cone that she glided back on to the bike path without looking where she was going. Before she realised what was happening, she saw a motorbike coming right at her!

She did her best to keep ahead of it, and she thought she'd be OK if the motorbike could somehow manage to swerve out of her way. But that was not the case because suddenly her purse flew out and hooked itself on one of the handlebars! Suddenly, Hay Lin was attached to a moving motorbike!

Hay Lin was terrified.

If only I'd worn my helmet, she thought despairingly. Who will I call if I have an accident? The motorbike's brakes were screeching; Hay Lin was sure she'd be flung into the bushes when the bike finally stopped.

Hay Lin crashed to the ground, somehow managing to hold on to her ice-cream cone! She wasn't hurt, but she was *totally* mortified.

The rider of the motorbike rushed over to her. "Are you still in one piece?" he asked.

Hay Lin avoided making eye contact. "Yeah? Why? Want to take another shot at me?" she said, trying to lighten things up. She saw a flash of concerned brown eyes, and she looked down at her legs and said, "I don't think anything's broken." To herself, she added, I need to get out of here. Right now!

The bike-rider's voice sounded genuinely worried. "Are you sure?" he asked her. "Is there anything I can do?"

"No, really . . . I'm OK," Hay Lin stammered. She just wanted the episode to be over. And then . . . she really looked at him for the first time.

The guy was just about her age. He had thick, dark, wavy hair and soft brown eyes that were completely focused on her at the moment. Hay Lin knew it was corny, but she couldn't help it . . . the guy's friendly smile took her breath away.

"Here, let me help you up," he said, extending his hand. After looking into his eyes, Hay Lin wasn't sure her legs were strong enough to hold her, but she took the boy's hand. She could have sworn that sparks flew. "Uh, yeah, thanks," she said. She didn't want to let go.

"Hey, you OK?" he asked again. "Man, what a fall!"

Hay Lin felt her face turning scarlet. With a big goofy smile, she replied, "Everything's fine, thanks," as politely as she could.

Maybe the guy was fooled into thinking she wasn't flustered by having a near-death experience and holding a cute guy's hand, all within a matter of seconds. But the rider of the motorbike quickly found out just how flustered she was, because somehow Hay Lin finally let go of her ice-cream cone! With a *splat* it crashed into the guy's shirt and slowly dripped down on to his shorts. Hay Lin's jaw dropped as the cute guy began to laugh. "Unbelievable!" he said. "Unbelievable!" He didn't seem bothered, but Hay Lin was.

"Unbelievable" is right, she thought. Why do things like that *always* happen to me?

She pretended to laugh, too, and then backed out of the park as quickly as she could, apologising over and over. Talk about an awkward encounter.

The whole way home she thought about the

incident and what her friends would have done. Cornelia would have asked the guy's name even after she'd covered him with ice cream. Irma probably would have gotten his phone number.

I'm hopeless! Hay Lin thought. She almost wished that the encounter in the park had never happened. She wanted to see the boy again . . . but even if she had known how to find him, it would have been too humiliating.

Hay Lin wondered how her friends always knew what to do when boys were around. Hay Lin liked being the independent one – she'd never wanted to be tied down by a boyfriend. But while she had been happy with her independence, her friends had been busy figuring out the boy situation.

And it's not like we weren't also busy with other things, Hay Lin reminded herself. How do they manage to fit it all in?

On top of all the usual stuff that mattered to girls their age, they were supposed to save the world! It made dealing with boys seem super easy.

It wasn't very long ago that the five friends had hardly known one another. Will and

Taranee had been new in town and immediately drawn to the others, but they had only just started hanging out together when Hay Lin's grandmother had made a big announcement out of the blue: the five of them hadn't met by *accident* – they were *destined* to be friends. That was because they'd been anointed as the next Guardians of the Veil by the Oracle, a man who lived in a place in the middle of infinity called Candracar.

Many centuries before, the Oracle had erected an invisible barrier, called the Veil, between the peaceful earth and a troubled world called Metamoor. Since then, the dark forces of Metamoor had tried many times to pierce the Veil, but the barrier had always held them back . . . until recently.

With the coming of the new millennium, weak spots had developed in the Veil, and openings, called portals, had opened between the two worlds. Unless something prevented it, the earth would be overrun by the evil that had been contained for so long. And that would be seriously bad news.

The girls' first job as Guardians was to close the portals. It sounded just about impossible, until the girls learned two things. First, the portals were all located in their hometown of Heatherfield, which meant they could work for the Oracle without blowing their cover. And second, the Oracle had anointed the girls with special powers to help them get the job done. Each of them would control one of the elements of nature!

Hay Lin had power over the air, which fit her perfectly. With her magic, she could float on the air and whip up a breeze whenever she chose to. Solid and logical Cornelia controlled the earth, while cool, quiet Taranee revealed her hotter side with her utter mastery over fire. Irma's magic controlled water. Just like one of Irma's moods, water could go from a trickle to a flood in no time flat! And Will? Well . . . Will had the most amazing power of them all, the magic that brought all the others together. She controlled a luminescent pink orb called the Heart of Candracar, which appeared in her hand whenever she really needed it. While each of the girls could transform by herself into a Guardian, the magical orb made the girls stronger. Will's power was energy, and her power energised and united the girls. The Heart would kick their magic up a notch, and with it there was almost nothing the girls couldn't do.

The girls had even come up with a name for their group: W.I.T.C.H. It was an acronym composed of the first letters of each of their names. Then they had set out to close the portals and save the world – and they'd succeeded. They'd even brought down Metamoor's ruthless monarch, Prince Phobos. It had felt as if they were unstoppable!

Hay Lin's thoughts were interrupted when she noticed her friends staring at her. "And then?" Irma demanded.

"And then?" the rest repeated.

Hay Lin had been totally distracted for a minute. Her friends were anxiously waiting to hear what had happened with the guy in the park.

Hay Lin smiled. She couldn't wait to go on. This was the good part. "Well, we saw each other again that night," she said, blushing. What had happened next was a total surprise.

She was supposed to be working at her family's restaurant, the Silver Dragon, that night, but calling it work was a stretch – there wasn't a customer in sight. Hay Lin stood behind a counter, reading a book and waiting by the phone for take-out orders. It was hot so close to the kitchen, but Hay Lin had a handheld fan to keep her cool. The fan's whirring sound also helped block out the clatter of pots and pans from the kitchen behind her, where the cook, Fang, was cleaning up.

The kitchen door swung open, and Fang came out, wiping his forehead with a towel. "You're still here?" he asked her. "Don't you know what's happening tonight?"

Hay Lin's eyes didn't leave her book. "Um," she murmured, "let me think." She didn't really want to be bothered. Whatever was happening outside the restaurant might as well have been happening on the moon. She'd promised her parents she'd work, and that was that. She had no intention of making other plans.

But the cook didn't seem to care what Hay Lin said. He started telling her about all the excitement she was missing on this paticularly *steamy* night. "They say the sky will be full of shooting stars!" he said proudly, as if he had put together the light show. "A dream will come true for each one you see."

Hay Lin thought of the guy from the park. "Sounds great," she said. Under her breath, she added, "There's a special wish *I'd* like to make." To run into that guy again . . . but not like the last time, she added to herself. Sighing, she put her book down on the counter, but its spine caught on a plastic tray, full of change that the last customer had left there, and sent it flying. "Oh, no!" Hay Lin said. She dived behind the counter to pick up the coins.

She was scrambling for the last few pennies when she heard someone walk into the restaurant and say, "How are you tonight?" The voice sounded familiar to Hay Lin, but it was speaking Chinese – a language she spoke only with her family. Who could it be?

"How are you tonight?" the voice repeated. Hay Lin was still trying to place it when she realised the voice was not directing itself at Fang but at *her*, and she couldn't be rude to a customer – it was one of her family's cardinal rules. Hay Lin got up from the floor as gracefully as she could. "I'm fine, thanks," she replied, a bit coolly.

When she finally looked up at the customer, though, she almost landed on the floor again.

No wonder the voice was familiar. It belonged to the boy from the park! She had no idea how he'd tracked her down, but, there he was, gazing at her shyly . . . and sweetly.

"Oh, great!" he said. He continued in Chinese. He was inviting her on the date of her dreams. "Want to go and count the shooting stars?" he asked finally in English.

Hay Lin was speechless for a second, but Fang filled in the silence. The cook stood behind the boy, gaping in surprise. "Who is he?" he whispered loudly in what he must have *thought* was a subtle way.

"Fang, this is . . . um . . ." Hay Lin stammered. She stumbled over his name, embarrassed because she clearly didn't know it.

"Eric Lyndon," the guy said after watching Hay Lin flail about. Then he added, "Pleased to meet you," and extended his hand to Fang.

The cook wasn't known for being friendly – he always said that the kitchen was the best part of the restaurant because it was farthest from the customers. But Hay Lin could tell he was intrigued by Eric. Fang squinted and stuck his nose in the air as he considered the boy. "So the young man speaks Chinese," he said. "Good going, Hay Lin!"

Hay Lin could feel her face turning red. "Fang!" she cautioned him.

"I only know a few words, and my accent is terrible," Eric Lyndon said modestly.

Suddenly, Fang was in a joking mood and pretended to be reading a fortune from a fortune cookie. "Wise man says, 'The accent is not important if the grammar is flawless.'" In his normal voice, he added, "What *is* important is that you get Hay Lin back on time." He smiled at Hay Lin and, when Eric's back was turned, winked.

The Guardian knew exactly what Fang was getting at. He's letting me go out on this date! she realised. And *nobody* needs to know!

A minute ago, Hay Lin had been resigned to spending the evening in the restaurant reading alone while shooting stars were lighting up the night sky. Now she was about to go out and watch them streak through the darkness with a mysterious boy who spoke her language . . . literally!

Hay Lin, let's get out of here quick! Hay Lin said to herself. She felt a little nervous about being alone with Eric, but she also felt strangely bold. Smiling, she grabbed his arm and said, "Let's get out of here, quick!"

Turning around, she caught Fang's eye and winked back at him. She would make it up to Fang somehow, but right now she wasn't going to worry about him closing the restaurant up by himself. "Thanks, Fang! Tell Mum and Dad I'll be back soon!" she said. Hay Lin stopped talking and sighed. She had told her friends the whole story and was almost afraid to meet their eyes. Her date with Eric had been perfect, and the only thing that could have made her happier would have been to see more of him at school that year! But what if that's all it was? One perfect night? Hay Lin worried that she'd missed some warning sign. What did it mean that he'd asked her out? Hay Lin thought that it probably meant that Eric liked her . . . but was there another way to see it?

Hay Lin crossed her fingers behind her back for good luck, then looked right at Cornelia, who was the most knowledgeable of all the girls on the subject of boys. And when she grinned back, Hay Lin's heart lifted, because all she needed to know was right there in her friend's happy look. Hay Lin was overjoyed to have a crush on Eric, but she was even more grateful to have friends like these. W.I.T.C.H. would be with Hay Lin in matters of love . . . just as it was in everything else.

TWO

Cornelia could practically feel the energy in the air as she walked towards the Sheffield Institute – or, the Sheffield Institution, to those in the know. Kids were thronging from all directions towards the big stone building. Its golden gates had been thrown open to the returning students and the clock over the entryway was ticking away the last moments of summer vacation. Nobody would be happy to see the summer end, but there was something exciting nonetheless about the first day of school. It was a whole new start. Anything could happen.

But it's all downhill from here, Cornelia reminded herself. Today people are tanned and relaxed and dressed up in summer styles. This time next week, though, there will already be a routine in place. It will seem like the summer never even happened!

Cornelia wasn't looking forward to sitting in classrooms or taking tests. But school had never been very hard for her. For one thing, she was a straight-A student. And for another, she'd always belonged to the school's popular crowd, the Infielders. Compared to the way it was for some other kids, school was a breeze for Cornelia.

It's funny how I don't care about that stuff any more, though, she thought. Hanging out with the cool kids and all that seems silly. Popularity contests and being in on all the latest gossip is a thing of the past for me. The only thing that matters is that I'm with my true friends now – the Guardians.

She suddenly had the weird feeling that the *summer* had been long and hard and that *school* would be a welcome refuge. In fact, the summer felt like a complete blur. Cornelia shook her head and tried to clear her mind.

Uncharacteristically, Irma was leading the way towards the school doors. As usual, though, she was also goofing off, pretending she was the cook from Hay Lin's restaurant. "Wise man says, 'If Hay Lin doesn't go to Eric, Eric will go to Silver Dragon,'" Irma said in a silly voice, holding two pencils to her nose in an imitation of Fang's mustache.

"Ha-ha! Cut it out, Irma!" laughed Taranee.

Cornelia smiled. Sometimes Irma could really crack her up – but sometimes she bugged her a lot, too. This was a time for new beginnings, Cornelia remembered. The first day of school was a blank slate. She had a feeling *Irma* wouldn't be ready for a personality makeover anytime soon. Hay Lin, however, was definitely changing.

Now that Hay Lin had told them her story about Eric, she lingered towards the back of the group, almost as if she were nervous. Her head was down, and she was playing with a loose strand of hair.

Cornelia waited for Hay Lin to catch up. "Shooting stars . . . wishes . . ." she said to her friend with a nudge. "Are you leaving anything out about that night?" Cornelia had read enough books to know how important it was to analyse every detail when it came to dates. Plus, she was dying to know what *exactly* happened next. Had Eric kissed Hay Lin? Had she seen him again after that night?

Starry-eyed, her friend responded, "We're just good friends is all! He told me such wonderful stories. . . ."

Did Hay Lin really believe what she was saying? Cornelia asked herself. She could claim all she wanted that she and Eric were just friends, but Cornelia detected a different note in Hay Lin's voice whenever she mentioned his name. She's smitten, Cornelia decided. But maybe a little afraid to admit it.

"Did you know that the heavenly vault is divided into eighty-eight sectors, corresponding to exactly that number of constellations?" Hay Lin asked dreamily.

Irma turned around. "Of course I know that!" she said. "Who doesn't?"

Her friends gave her a doubtful look. They knew Irma too well to fall for the little lie.

"Really, I did!" Irma insisted, rolling her eyes.

Cornelia almost started laughing at Hay Lin's random factoid – until she realised it must have had something to do with Eric. She fell into step with her friend as Hay Lin finished describing the details of their date.

"Eric had just arrived in Heatherfield," Hay Lin explained. "We went to the observatory, where he lives with his grandfather, Professor Zachary Lyndon."

The name didn't sound familiar to Cornelia. But she'd seen the observatory on the edge of town – a small, domed building on a bluff near the water. She'd seen seagulls swarming around it, but never any people there.

It's probably a great place to see the stars, Cornelia thought. It's isolated and far from the lights of the city. The only noise would be the sound of each other's heartbeats. Talk about romantic!

It made Cornelia happy to think of her friend basking in starlight on an empty rooftop with a boy she liked. And it gave her a little thrill to think of Hay Lin crushing on this mysterious stranger, Eric. Hay Lin sort of floated through life – it could be hard to get close to her, hard to pin her down.

If she's falling for this boy, though, we'll have something new in common, Cornelia thought. Something else to draw us together besides the whole Guardian thing.

Hay Lin's voice still sounded dreamy as she continued to talk about Eric. "He told me about the stars and about all the trips he's been on. It's amazing! He's lived with his parents *all* over the world!"

Which could be why he speaks Chinese, Cornelia noted silently. With all that travelling, he was bound to pick up a few things – like foreign languages.

"He's been to such fascinating places," Hay Lin continued. "And he sees the good in all of them. His stories could make anyone believe that suffering doesn't exist in the world!"

It took Cornelia a moment to wrap her mind around that one. And when she did, she found herself getting all philosophical. She felt certain that, no matter what Eric had told Hay Lin, suffering did exist. Someplace else. Or was it closer? Cornelia knew she led a charmed life in Heatherfield, and yet when Hay Lin said, "suffering," the word resonated in Cornelia's soul. It was as if she'd experienced it herself . . . only she was sure she hadn't.

Some people believe in past lives, Cornelia thought. Maybe that is what is going on – something awful happened to me long ago. Or was something happening on the other side of the universe reverberating inside me for some reason that no one can explain? Am I feeling someone else's suffering?

Cornelia moved away from the cosmic questions with her usual self-discipline. This was Hay Lin's moment, and she deserved Cornelia's complete attention.

How magnificent it would be to gaze into the night sky, she thought, and to see the Milky Way through an expert's eyes! As the earth girl in her group, Cornelia was totally grounded. But something in Hay Lin's story made her long to lose herself in the stars, to travel across galaxies to something – or someone – far away. . . .

Again, Cornelia's thoughts ground to a halt. What was going on? she wondered. What did she need to escape from? She'd never had mixed feelings at the start of a school year before. She was usually excited to start. But this time, it was as if she had unfinished business. But what could it be? Cornelia asked herself. Was it something to do with this summer?

Come to think of it, she realised, it was hard to remember the summer at all. She recalled spending a week with her friends at Camp Cormoran, where Irma's family had rented a cabin. Then her dad had picked her up and driven her back to Heatherfield. And soon after that, the Hale family had embarked on another vacation, this one at Riddlescott Lake. They'd had a splendid house on the water; Cornelia had loved it there.

As she and her friends entered the crowd of students inside the gates, Cornelia thought of the summer scrapbook she'd just put together. There were photos in it, of Irma making funny faces for the camera, of Will glued to her cell phone on the beach, of Taranee with her brother in the mountain town of Sesamo, of Hay Lin fast asleep. There were postcards her friends had sent her when they had been separated, and mementos from their time together, like chopsticks from the Silver Dragon and ticket stubs from a concert. Suddenly Cornelia was glad she had put it all together. That was what a scrapbook is for, she thought. To preserve memories. And it looks like I'm going to need all the help I can get! Because I can't seem to remember everything.

Cornelia felt sure the details would come

flooding back once she looked at her scrapbook again. Then she would turn them over and over in her mind as she sat in class, thinking longingly of her weeks of leisure.

Anyway, she thought, my memory had better sharpen up before my first test is scheduled. Otherwise, this school year will be a lot tougher than I thought!

THREE

Yan Lin shook her head slowly as she observed the Guardians in Heatherfield, beginning their new year at school. It was not very long ago that she'd lived with Hay Lin's family above the Silver Dragon and taken great pride in getting her granddaughter ready for the first day of school.

Yan Lin fondly remembered the way she would fuss over the girl's outfit and braid her hair. She would put a special treat in Hay Lin's lunch box and wave to her until the girl disappeared into a crowd of children at the street corner.

How long ago all that seemed! Yan Lin thought wistfully. And how much had changed since then! So many things had happened to her granddaughter – some good, some bad.

Just like her granddaughter, Yan Lin had once been a Guardian. She served Candracar even now, but in a different way: when Yan Lin's life on the earth had ended, she had come to Candracar to serve as one of the Oracle's most trusted advisers. Yan Lin was grateful for the way she could help the Oracle while continuing to keep an eye on Hay Lin from this magnificent, magical place. But just then, she was deeply concerned about the young Guardians.

The girls had triumphed in closing the portals and restoring the rightful heir to the throne in Metamoor. But lately it had become clear to those in Candracar what the Guardians' next mission would be, and the news had Yan Lin extremely worried.

The Guardians were to face a new foe – Nerissa. And Nerissa was far more devious and destructive than Prince Phobos. If she had her way and got her hands on their powers, Nerissa would be able to use them with devastating force against the girls . . . and Candracar! She was a horrifying force and one which the

Guardians should never have had to face.

Yan Lin sighed. I hope the Oracle knows what he is doing, she thought. There is so much riding on his decision . . . so many lives.

It was not like her to question his decisions, but this time she had her doubts about his latest plan for the Guardians. He had arranged for their memories to be wiped clean for a while, until he deemed them ready to face Nerissa. The Oracle was all-knowing and all-powerful, but once in a great while he made a mistake.

What if he is making a mistake this time? Yan Lin wondered anxiously. What if he is unwittingly putting Hay Lin and her friends in harm's way by erasing all they have been through with Nerissa this summer?

The possibility made Yan Lin shiver with fear. She, of all people, knew Nerissa's strength. She had once been her fellow Guardian, and Yan Lin had been witness to her downfall. What if the Oracle had underestimated Nerissa's thirst for revenge? Or, her pure evil nature.

Yan Lin had hoped the girls would get a breather after their first mission. But that was not to be the case.

Nerissa's evil had crept into their summer vacation. Nerissa had found the Guardians and invaded their dreams, making sleep a nightmare. And she had actually made contact with the girls. It would not be long before her shadow fell over their school year as well.

It is all in the life of a Guardian, Yan Lin reminded herself, to bounce from one crisis to another. But she remembered the aftermath of the young Guardians' first mission all too well. It had taken quite a toll on the five girls. Their friendship had almost been destroyed.

After the Guardians had closed the portals in the Veil, they had returned to Heatherfield, divided. In Metamoor, yes, they had worked as a team to defeat the ruthless prince. They had also worked with the rebel forces, led by a young hero named Caleb.

Once, Caleb had been a type of flower in one of Phobos's extensive gardens. These flowers were the Murmurers, the eyes and ears of the kingdom – the prince's informants. Caleb, through the sheer force of his will, became a boy again, and then a leader of the rebels. With his good looks and brave personality, he made a great leader. When Cornelia met him, it was love at first sight – though she had actually seen him in her dreams before.

There was no law against a Guardian's falling in love. But Cornelia took a grave risk in loving a boy who had, after all, once been on the other side.

Prince Phobos also felt strongly about Caleb . . . in a completely opposite way. He reserved a special hatred for him, and his last act as the ruler of Metamoor was to turn Caleb back into a flower!

When she returned home, Cornelia was absolutely crushed. She'd smuggled Caleb, in flower form, back to Heatherfield and vowed never to leave his side – even if it meant being separated from her friends. She was over-whelmed with grief, and couldn't deal with any-one – even her closest friends. Slowly, she pulled further and further away.

Cornelia's distancing herself from the group created a horrible domino effect. Before long, none of the girls wanted to be together – and when they managed to be in the same place at the same time, they bickered. But this was only the beginning of a much bigger disaster, Yan Lin remembered. Even the Oracle had no way to know what forces were about to be unleashed by the girls' division and anger.

In Candracar, the girls' powers were represented by five droplets of magical essence, called the Aurameres. These essences existed in the Aura Hall, where they spun constantly and were observed at all times by Luba, the Keeper of the Aurameres. She could not help noticing that the Aurameres shrank in size as the girls' friendship grew more troubled. But did Luba do anything? No!

The memory of it made Yan Lin flush with anger. Since the Guardians had been chosen, Luba had always had her doubts about them, and a wish to see them replaced. The Aurameres were her means of making that happen. So she sat back and allowed the Aurameres to dwindle until the girls' powers were gone. It was all part of her plan. Then she went ahead and interfered inexcusably. She fused four of the Aurameres together!

In doing so, Luba created a monster called an Altermere. It combined the powers of Will, Irma, Hay Lin, and Taranee – and its ultimate goal was to assume Cornelia's power as well. When it eventually did find her, the Altermere was absorbed by Cornelia. Without knowing it, the blonde Guardian suddenly gained control of the five great powers of the universe: earth, air, fire, water, and energy.

Yan Lin still found it astounding that the Keeper of the Aurameres would conspire against the Guardians or that the five great powers would be combined – and there would be worse to come. When the powers became one, terrible forces were unleashed in the world. The presence of those forces released Candracar's greatest traitor, Nerissa, from her eternal punishment in the depths of Mount Thanos!

Yan Lin had feared this catastrophe since the moment Nerissa had been sentenced so long ago. It had come to pass, in part, because the new Guardians had grown distant from one another. Their anger had set the stage and made room for Nerissa's return. While Yan Lin trusted the girls, she wondered if they would be able to work together in the same way now as they always had before. They had to set things right and become a group again. As her mind drifted back to the rest of Caleb's – and Cornelia's – story, she pushed the concern from her mind.

Of course, Cornelia had no idea that the natural order of things had been disturbed or that the infamous Nerissa had therefore been set free. She had no idea that at that very moment she possessed all of the Guardians' powers and could do almost anything. Cornelia was focused on only one thing: Caleb. She had a feeling that she could bring Caleb back to human form. Little did she know that there was a power pulsating through her body that could make that dream a reality. Finally, however, she was able to do the one thing she had been longing for – she brought him back!

Luba attempted to punish Cornelia for reviving Caleb. It was as if she couldn't stop going after the Guardians. So she had her brought to trial before the Council of Elders in Candracar. The Council was about to deliberate when Caleb himself stepped in. He would stay in Candracar forever, he said, if Cornelia were set free.

Caleb's sacrifice allowed Cornelia to return to Heatherfield to be with her friends. Surely it was painful for the young lovers to be separated, but the Guardians were united again, which was more important, especially now that Nerissa had begun to stage her revenge against Candracar!

Nerissa's first act had been to create some monstrous servants to do her bidding. She used them to track down the Guardians and uncover their weaknesses. And once she had learned the story of Caleb, she zeroed in on him as her first victim. He had held a copy of the five great powers since the time when Cornelia used them to bring him back to human form. With those powers in her own hands, Nerissa knew, she would be able to battle the Guardians on equal terms.

But Nerissa wasn't the only one who was after Caleb.

Luba, too, was ready to pounce. She'd left Candracar in disgrace, determined to oust the Guardians – or at least to clear her name. She could not allow the Guardians to continue to make her into the fool. Luba knew that the Oracle would send Caleb, as his Herald of Candracar, to earth to find her. So Luba lay in wait, disguised as a friend of Cornelia's family, hoping that Caleb would not be able to resist making a side trip to see his beloved. Then she would have them both in one place. Caleb walked right into her trap on the shores of Riddlescott Lake, where the Hales were on vacation. The moment she saw Caleb, Luba brought him down – until she, in turn, was brought down by Nerissa's minions!

The Guardians got there in time to fend off Nerissa's forces before they could do more harm – but failed to protect Caleb, who was whisked away by the fearsome creatures. By the time they arrived in Candracar, demanding an explanation, the five girls were devastated and drained.

Yan Lin remembered how they had stood before the Oracle, and she could still see their long faces as they heard his somber words of warning.

"Her name is Nerissa," the Oracle had begun slowly. "She was a Guardian before she betrayed Candracar and her friends." He looked soberly at the girls and added, "Now that she has captured Caleb, and his copy of your five powers, we are all in danger!"

Irma threw up her hands. "I thought we were on vacation!" she cried. "Sunshine, the seaside, sleeping late . . . jeez! When can we leave to get this Nerissa?"

"Not yet," the Oracle cautioned.

But Cornelia was impatient and tired of constantly being kept away from Caleb. "What do you mean, 'not yet'? You said it yourself. . . . She's dangerous!" she said. "I'm not going to just stand around waiting for her to hurt Caleb!"

Yan Lin understood Cornelia's impatience. But her position was to support the Oracle. Her role was to help him carry out his plan. So she had had to interject, loyally. "You will do nothing!" she told the girls. "You faced Nerissa's emissaries at Riddlescott Lake, and you were saved only because her objective was something different!"

It was the truth. Nerissa's servants lacked the magic that the girls held, but they had more than enough brute strength to compensate. Nerissa had formed her monsters from the only materials available to her at the ends of the earth. Ember and Tridart were winged creatures, transparent but lethal, who embodied the terrifying properties of fire and ice. And Shagon, with his long and snaking hair, his muscle-bound body, was the personification of hate itself. It was indeed fortunate that they had come for Caleb and not for the Guardians. And it was a great coincidence that Luba had been there, too, to absorb some of Nerissa's rage.

They will not be so lucky the next time, Yan Lin thought. Which is why they need to be as prepared as possible!

Of course, she had not foreseen the Oracle's plan to clear their minds for a while. Yet she could do nothing but be supportive once his decision was made. "Trust in us, Hay Lin," Yan Lin had said to her granddaughter, almost as if she were trying to persuade herself. "The Oracle's wisdom is infinite."

Hay Lin's reaction was unsurprising. She drew her hands to her chest and asked the Oracle, "And Caleb? He's all alone, and he needs us!" Her devotion to Caleb's safety made her grandmother proud.

"The glory of some is found in sacrifice," the Oracle replied, folding his hands.

Cornelia glared at him. "This is out of control," she shot back. "We've been fighting your battles, and now you want to stop us from helping our friend?"

Yan Lin drew in her breath. How would the Oracle respond to such impertinence? It was so uncharacteristic of the Guardians.

"Those battles were not only ours, Cornelia," he said wisely. "You saved Candracar and Metamoor. Even Heatherfield!" He was patient with her insolence, but he was unmoved by her argument. The Oracle's gaze met Cornelia's; finally her eyes dropped to the floor. "Now, go!" the Oracle ordered softly. "No one can foresee what destiny holds in store! No one!"

Yan Lin came back to the present. The destiny the Oracle had in mind for them now was selective amnesia.

Perhaps the Oracle considers it a chance for the girls to rest and recuperate for the many battles yet to come, she thought. And perhaps his strategy is right. He had always been wise and just. I just hope that he has thought this through. Because right now the five girls do not remember Caleb nor the threat of Nerissa's evil plan.

If there was one thing Yan Lin knew for sure, it was that Nerissa would not ease up in her pursuit of revenge. As the forgetful

Guardians awaited the Oracle's next orders, Nerissa would be drawing ever close to them. And the experiences that had drawn the girls together would be of no help then, since they would remember nothing of their last mission. Would they be able to stick together? she wondered. Yan Lin trusted the girls, but she was worried about Nerissa. More than anyone else, Yan Lin knew the consequences of a rift between Guardians. And she knew for certain that the universe would be destroyed if it happened again.

FOUR

Deep inside the Temple of Candracar, the Oracle took a gulp of air and held it in his lungs for a long time before letting it out. Then he closed his eyes and began again, breathing deeply and trying to clear his mind. It had been a long time, perhaps centuries, since the Oracle had felt so rattled. The Guardians he had chosen were up against forces he had never thought they would have to face . . . at least not this soon. The Oracle was all-knowing and all-powerful, but even he could not have predicted the cataclysm that ensued when Cornelia absorbed the Altermere. No matter how regular his breathing or how still his posture, his best efforts at meditation were failing.

His pulse raced. He hoped he had made the right choices to help the five girls defeat Nerissa.

The Guardians are the only ones who can face her evil, the Oracle thought. Their powers are awesome and their bond is strong.

But Nerissa's desire for revenge is so ferocious that I fear she has the capacity to crush them now, the Oracle thought. I will not allow them to meet her until they have every possible defense at their disposal. It would not be fair. We must all be patient as everything comes together, even if Nerissa grows stronger as a result of our delay. That is a risk, of course, but a risk we must take. There is no other option.

The Oracle felt confident of his decision, yet his most loyal advisers were questioning his judgment. If only I could explain to them, he thought, and set their minds at ease! But what he had in mind for the Guardians had to remain secret in order to be effective. He would have to face whatever criticism came his way, even if it were from his dearest friends and confidants.

When the Guardians had last left Candracar,

Yan Lin had stood beside him, watching the girls walk away with sagging shoulders and heavy hearts. "Do you really believe that they will wait and do nothing?" she had asked. Her voice was soft, but the glint in her eyes was not.

The Oracle knew that she was worried about the girls, especially Hay Lin; she wasn't sure she completely trusted his plan to tamper with their memories. The Oracle had led Yan Lin through the Great Hall, where bright sun streamed in through the tall, arched windows. Their footsteps echoed on the smooth marble floor and off the elaborate carvings all around them. There was no other noise in the Great Hall. Yan Lin followed the Oracle along a narrow catwalk that ended in a balcony from which they could see the glorious Temple spread out beneath them. It was only then, when they were alone, that the Oracle had responded to her question.

"If *you* were in their place, would *you* give up so easily?" he asked.

The view before them was majestic, with light dancing on the carvings and fountains feeding ponds of water lilies far below. Yan Lin was thinking, and closing her eyes to the beautiful surroundings. When she opened them, she admitted that the Oracle had a point. "No," she answered slowly, "I wouldn't."

"Exactly," the Oracle said. "It is our duty to protect them from themselves! At least for the time being, they mustn't think about Nerissa or Caleb. That is why I will cloud their memories. Caleb is a strong young man, Yan Lin. I know he will be able to wait it out." He was glad Yan Lin seemed to see the situation from his point of view. But still, the conversation put him on edge.

Yan Lin turned her eyes towards the sky. "I truly hope so," she said softly. "So, the Guardians will forget everything, then?" she asked after a moment of silence. "They'll lose *all* of their memories?"

The Oracle reassured her. "No," he explained. "Only those that are tied to Nerissa. And Caleb, I'm afraid."

At that moment, Tibor, another of the Oracle's inner circle, arrived with an important announcement. "Oracle!" he'd said urgently. "The prisoner has arrived, and the Council of Elders awaits you!"

With a quick glance at Yan Lin, the Oracle

had led the way from the balcony back into the Great Hall, where the Congregation had gathered yet again to weigh in on the fate of somebody its members knew well. This time it was not Cornelia, however. This time they would decide the fate of Luba herself, who had betrayed them all.

The thought of sentencing Luba made the Oracle's heart ache. He remembered the scene quite clearly.

Luba had guarded the Aurameres faithfully for centuries. The Oracle did not believe she had intended any of the things that had happened after she had fused them together. He'd been inclined to show her mercy, but it was more important to send a message about the consequences of interfering with the Guardians' work. The Oracle felt sorry for Luba, but he knew he would need to stay firm. He needed to remain the leader and to put his personal feelings aside.

The Congregation fell silent as the Oracle entered the chamber, scanning the benches to make sure that all of the Elders were accounted for. When the silence seemed more than anyone could bear, Luba finally appeared, dressed in the flowing red robes of the disgraced, her wrists encircled by chains. The Oracle had expected Luba to look contrite, but her expression was defiant.

"Luba!" he cried, "Behold the face of him who, because of you, is now in danger!"

He'd gestured towards the air, where a window had opened on to a terrible scene on the other side of the universe. There was Caleb, in Nerissa's clutches, imprisoned and alone. There was the boy who had helped regain Metamoor from Prince Phobos, the boy who had saved Cornelia, *and* pledged his loyalty to Candracar. It made the Oracle angry to think of how Luba's mistake had cost this young man his freedom. There must be justice, the Oracle told himself. Whatever Luba's history, she must pay for this crime against the Guardians. She must pay for the misery that Nerissa would bring upon them all because of the poor judgment of the Keeper of the Aurameres!

The Oracle sighed. His heart was heavy. Luba needed to be punished, but the Oracle knew that Luba thought she was acting in good faith to save Candracar. While her actions were not right, her heart was in the right place. It was a very difficult time for the Oracle.

Tibor chose that moment of silence to shout, "Because of you, Luba, Nerissa's revenge will soon rage down upon Candracar, dragging us into a battle that we have never wished for – and that we may not be able to withstand!"

Luba's face was expressionless.

"What have you to say in your defense?" the Oracle demanded. She deserved one chance to speak in her own behalf, he thought.

But it seemed the Council disagreed. Another of the Elders bellowed, "No, Oracle, the time for words is over!" He did not care what Luba had to say in her own defense – he wanted to jump right to the sentencing. "This time, may the punishment be fitting!" he proclaimed. "The Congregation was merciful with Nerissa, and as a result, that creature has returned!"

"He's right," the Elders chorused. "Who will save us now?"

The Oracle winced. He did not feel that they had been merciful with Nerissa. She had been condemned for all eternity to the depths of

Mount Thanos, a volcano on the edge of a frozen tundra. Her powers were stripped from her, and she was sealed in a tomb in order that she might contemplate her mistakes in quarters she could never leave. Yes, the tomb would break apart if the five great powers of the universe were ever to be united. But nobody had ever expected that to happen. At the time, her sentence had been considered worse than death.

"Silence!" the Oracle ordered the Elders as Luba watched warily. He would not listen to any more of their second-guessing. "The sentence passed down on Nerissa was terrible, as befitted her crime!" The Elders glared at him, their arms folded in anger. "Must I remind you of how things unfolded?" he asked. It pained him to remember that dreadful day, yet he forced himself to recount it to the Elders once again.

The images penetrated his deepest meditative trance, seared into his mind and his memory. What I wouldn't give to erase those images as I will erase others from the young Guardians! he thought. The pain of carrying them inside was so great.

Again, the Oracle breathed deeply. Perhaps if he allowed the memories to play out in his mind they would cease to haunt him for the next few hours.

He told the Council the tale of Nerissa – who had been a Guardian herself: the Keeper of the Heart of Candracar. With her companions – Kadma, Halinor, Cassidy, and Yan Lin – she had carried out the Oracle's orders and helped to preserve all that Candracar stood for. Nerissa was able to marshal the Heart's power to do amazing things. But then, slowly, she was consumed and corrupted by its power. Before long she decided that she had to have the Heart's power all to herself!

The other Guardians tried to stop her, but their friendship meant nothing to Nerissa if it stood between her and the Heart. In a deadly battle, Nerissa killed Cassidy, the youngest member of the group. The Guardians managed to stop Nerissa from seizing the Heart, but they paid a terrible price . . . they lost two friends in one battle.

And Nerissa paid a price as well, the Oracle reminded himself – no matter what the Congregation said.

Nerissa had stood before him as Luba would one day do, bound by chains and furious. She had insisted on wearing a bright purple gown, regal and proud even in her most angry moment; her long, curly hair danced in the breeze around her. The Oracle stood before her, unfurled the scroll of Candracar, and read to Nerissa what he had written: the particulars of her punishment. "Confined within the depths of Mount Thanos," he said, "deprived of her powers, with neither aid nor companionship. That is our decision!" he finished with a flourish.

Nerissa had stared at him, her eyes blazing, then raised her fist in the air. "This is a bad decision!" she'd shouted in disgust. "A horrible mistake!" Her voice grew low as she threatened, "I will return, I promise, and you will all regret having stood in my way, mark my words!"

Watching Nerissa leave the chamber that day, the Oracle had thought his heart would break. He had chosen her to wield the Heart, and at one time he had been pleased by the way she used her power. If it pained him to see her destruction, however, he had only to look at the remaining Guardians to remind himself of the reason it was necessary. Kadma, Halinor, and young Yan Lin were all that remained of the original five. The Oracle stumbled for something to say to them. "Cassidy sacrificed herself to protect Candracar!" he said finally. "Now it is up to all of us to protect the Heart!" But even to the Oracle, the words sounded hollow. They didn't seem like enough, given all that the Guardians had been through.

But once again, the three girls had impressed him. Yan Lin had stepped forward, holding the Heart gingerly, since she was not yet used to handling it. "Of course, Oracle," she'd whispered. "We have lost two friends, yet we will dry our tears and serve the Temple!"

The original Guardians' courage and dignity had inspired the Oracle for many years after that. Even without their friends, they had carried on their work and remained faithful to the Temple. And now, thought the Oracle fondly, one has even passed the tradition on to her own granddaughter! Hay Lin had inherited many of Yan Lin's best traits.

The Oracle exhaled with more force than he had been able to muster all morning. If the new

Guardians are anything like the old, he thought, they will find the strength to face whatever crosses their path – even if it is as evil as Nerissa. I cannot do their work for them, but it is my responsibility to keep them as safe as I can.

The Oracle rubbed his chin thoughtfully. That is why it was right to be harsh with Luba, he told himself. He had to make this situation right again.

FIVE

As night fell, Caleb huddled deeper inside his hooded cloak and put his head in his hands. He had no idea how long he'd been waiting to be rescued, but he was beginning to worry that he wouldn't be able to wait much longer. He was growing weak.

After striking him unconscious and abducting him from Riddlescott Lake, Nerissa's helpers had dropped him into a frozen wasteland that stretched in every direction, as far as he could see. Now Caleb was in a cave, surrounded by towering icicles and wide expanses of snow. He was utterly alone, except for a rumbling volcano on the horizon. Caleb thought that he might be on Mount Thanos, where Nerissa had once been sentenced to live for all eternity, but he wasn't sure. The thought of it would have been enough to make Caleb shiver if he hadn't been shivering already.

She is getting ready to pounce, he thought. Preparing to harm my friends – and Cornelia. The love of my life.

Just then, the volcano roared menacingly and belched out boiling lava. That happened every once in a while, but what would it be like when it *really* erupted? Caleb wondered, trying to think of an escape plan. What would it be like when the volcano – and Nerissa's rage – finally exploded?

He hoped to be far away by then, ready to help the Guardians fend Nerissa off.

But first they have to find me, Caleb thought.

While he was disappointed that the Guardians were not there to help, Caleb thought that maybe they didn't know what was going on. They should have been there by now, said a doubting voice inside his head. Had they forgotten him altogether? After all, they'd worked side by side to save the city of Meridian and replace the brutal Prince Phobos with the rightful queen, Elyon. They had made the perfect team.

He remembered the way Cornelia had cared for him so lovingly when he was in his flower form. She had never left him alone. She never stopped believing that he could be restored to the form of the boy she loved.

Caleb straightened up and gathered his strength. He would need to do this on his own. Like the many rebel attacks that he had planned in Meridian against Phobos and his army, Caleb would need to be brave now. He needed to show Nerissa that he was not afraid. He had to devise a plan of escape.

A sudden pain shot through Caleb. What if something had happened to the Guardians? To Cornelia? The last time he had seen her, she was fighting against Nerissa's minions.

It was hard to think about, but at that point nothing seemed impossible to Caleb. After all, who would ever have thought that Nerissa would return, or that he, a former Murmurer, would now possess a copy of the five great powers that she was so hungry to take? Who would ever have thought that he, once a heroic leader, could be so vulnerable now?

The Oracle had sent Caleb, as the Herald of Candracar, to earth with instructions to bring

Luba back to him. But Caleb didn't know how to control his magic yet, and Luba could sense it whenever he was drawing close to her. Somehow he had managed to track Will down. He would always be grateful for the way Will had snuck out of her house, no questions asked. She didn't laugh at him when she discovered he'd failed to master earthly skills like reading maps or riding the motorcycle he had borrowed. And she had led him right to Riddlescott Lake, right to Cornelia, and right to Luba herself.

Caleb rubbed his hands together to warm them. He almost wished the volcano would spurt out some more lava, deadly as it was. At least, when the lava hit it, the ice melted, which gave Caleb some water to drink and a patch of warmth to sleep on until the lava was covered by a fresh layer of ice. He hadn't had water or rest in many hours now.

He was hovering near unconsciousness when he suddenly felt as though he weren't alone.

It was a woman. Or, to be more specific, it *had* been a woman once – now she was more like a skeleton. Her face looked like a skull, with leathery skin stretched tight over her sharp features. Her hair fell almost to her knees in stringy curls, and her emaciated body was hidden in the folds of a tattered purple robe. The woman's eyes gleamed at him maniacally, and her lips were pulled back in a cruel smile that exposed every one of her rotten teeth.

"Well, well, well," she said. "Well, well, well." She stared at him for a long time, as if transfixed by the sight.

Caleb drew away from her instinctively. "Who are you?" he demanded.

"You disappoint me, Caleb," croaked the woman. "Don't you recognise me?" When Caleb failed to answer, she cackled, "I am Nerissa! Nerissa, who has returned to claim what belongs to her!" Then she collapsed into a fit of raspy, mirthless laughter.

This . . . this . . . creature is Nerissa, he thought suddenly. Right here in front of me. What am I supposed to do? What is it that she wants from me?

He summoned all the strength that he had, and stood up.

Nerissa gripped his chin between her bony fingers, as if she had read his mind. "I need the powers that you now hold!" she shrieked.

Filling himself up with as much confidence as he could muster, Caleb shot back, "You'll get nothing from me!"

"Are you so sure?" Nerissa sneered.

A steely determination flooded back into Caleb in spite of his desolation. I can hold her off for a while, he realised. At least until help comes. I will *never* give her what she wants, since it is clear she'll use it to hurt Cornelia and the other Guardians.

He loved Cornelia too much to let harm come to her if he could prevent it. "Want to find out just how little I'll give you?" Caleb taunted Nerissa. "Then go ahead and try me!"

The former Guardian grasped her staff, which was twisted at one end into a strange symbol – a half-moon crossed by a jagged bolt of lightning. Caleb could hear her muttering to herself as her fingers wound around it. "I have to admit that I've gotten a bit rusty lately," she said. "But they say that it's like riding a bicycle. Once you learn to be evil, you never forget how it's done!" Again she bent over and was consumed with laughter at her own pitiful joke.

Caleb felt himself strangely drawn to the dry

and hideous sound . . . which was how Nerissa caught him completely off guard!

With no warning, Nerissa whirled around and thrust her staff into the air, conjuring up a blinding light. *Kra-ack!* It blasted at Caleb, knocking him backwards. He took a few steps to gain his balance, but he couldn't see, nor fight back against Nerissa. She was lost in the blazing light, her magic searing the air and the ground.

The ice under Caleb's feet began to melt with the heat generated by Nerissa's power. And the lava beneath was more than just exposed – it was restored to life! *Blublublub*, it burbled, gathering around his feet. Soon Caleb was dancing to avoid it, his head still frozen solid while his feet felt as though they were being burned to a crisp.

Suddenly, Nerissa's face was mere inches away from his. "I didn't grant you permission to move!" she screeched. The light faded, and Caleb's eyes adjusted. Before him stood Nerissa, looking as though she were electrified with rage. And behind her was a group of monsters, her private army. Caleb had had a glimpse of them before: the glowing red woman with the metal blades for wings called Ember, the blue thug called Tridart, and the masked avenger with snakes for hair named Shagon.

"I still have to introduce you to my friends," Nerissa gloated. Then she shook her head. "How foolish of me!" she corrected herself, feigning innocence. "You've already met – in Riddlescott, isn't that right?"

She was right. In Riddlescott, Caleb had barely glanced at them before they'd knocked him to the ground, causing him to writhe in pain. Then, he had only the vaguest memory of them roughly transporting him to the ends of the earth. But that didn't matter now. He did not need to know them well to understand that they were fearsome and heartless. *And*, he was about to face them alone.

The bald one gurgled, "Urrrgh!" and the snake-haired guy responded "Nahrrr!" as if they were having a conversation about how to finish him off.

The monsters began to advance, and there was still no sign of the Guardians.

I'm trapped! Caleb thought.

"No!" he screamed as they closed in on him.

I have got to find a way to hold them off, he thought desperately. I'm just not sure I can do it by myself. But I know that I have to try. Hopefully help will come . . . soon.

SIX

Back in Heatherfield, another boy was waiting, too, searching for a particular redhead in the crowd of students gathered on the grounds of the Sheffield Institute. Matt stopped just short of the school's main gates to shift his messenger bag from one shoulder to another. He shook out his hair, still a little wet from the shower, and tried to decide what he'd say when he saw her.

"Hello, Will!" he thought he might say. That sounds like a teacher, he thought. It's no good at all.

He wanted to sound casual, since other people would be around. It wasn't the time or place to spill his guts or sound mushy and love-struck. On the other hand, he had to sound like more than just an acquaintance, he reasoned. He'd been thinking of nothing but Will all summer! He'd missed her more than she could ever have guessed. More than *he* thought was possible.

That was it! Matt realised. He knew what to say! He said it aloud to see how it felt on his tongue. "Will, I missed you!" he announced with a smile. Much better, he decided. Much better, indeed.

Now, if only he could find her. On a normal school day, kids got to school as late as they could without missing the bell. No one wanted to be caught looking *excited* about school. The first day of the school year was different, though. Everyone arrived early to catch up on the summer news before they were handed their books and their schedules and ushered into homeroom.

Everyone seemed to be grouping up in the usual formation. Matt could see all the jocks gathered at one corner of the lawn, tossing a Frisbee. He also spotted some guys he knew from his band, and the girl who'd been his lab partner last year in science class. But still no Will.

Where was she? he wondered a little anxiously. She'd told him about the way her mum's job had almost been transferred out of Heatherfield. That hadn't happened though, he remembered. So Will had to be there somewhere. He shielded his eyes from the sun and kept on looking.

He was totally nervous. Matt knew how he felt about Will – he was crazy about her. And she was so cool – she didn't mind that he'd forgotten his wallet when he took her out to the Lodelyday, the fanciest restaurant in town. She wasn't the kind of girl who cared about fine china or waiters in tuxedos. And she didn't seem to worry if plans changed. No, Will was just as happy at the Golden Diner, where they'd ended up, and she didn't even mind that she'd had to pay for his burger. Matt had never felt so comfortable on a first date, and he was still kicking himself for not kissing her when he walked her home.

There was still a big question in his mind, though: did Will feel the same way? Everything between them had been great during the week she had been at Irma's beach house. They'd traded flirtatious text messages all week long.

But when she got home, he'd called her house and gotten her mum's boyfriend (who also happened to be their history teacher, Mr. Collins – talk about awkward!) on the phone. Mr. Collins had told him that Will wasn't there, which was no big deal. But then he'd said he was looking out the window and watching Will get on the back of some boy's motorcycle! Matt had almost lost it, but instead he had just slammed the phone down.

For the next few weeks, Matt had tried to push that incident towards the back of his mind. He knew there'd been chemistry with Will at the restaurant and in their text messages. And they got along so well. But he couldn't help wondering – what if she liked someone else? What if she was just stringing him along? They were not quite going out, but that didn't mean she should have been seeing someone else behind his back, either. The insecurities drove Matt up the wall.

Unfortunately, the two of them hadn't had a chance to talk since Mr. Collins had ratted her out. Will had spent the rest of the summer with her mum at a remote resort with bad cell-phone reception. It had been impossible to get hold of her. Matt was excited to see her now, and willing to give her the benefit of the doubt.

But we definitely have to have a talk, he thought. And I'm not exactly looking forward to it. After all, she could have changed her mind over the summer. She could be over him!

Matt liked her so much that he wasn't sure he could handle a rejection.

His eyes scanned the crowd, and the knot in his stomach grew bigger as he continued not to spot Will with her usual crowd of friends. Then, all of a sudden, there they were!

Will was standing with Cornelia, Irma, Hay Lin, and Taranee on the other side of the school gate. There was a stranger with them, too, a guy with dark, wavy hair and a goofy smile, wearing a purple T-shirt. Matt didn't think much of this at first. Until he noticed that the guy was holding Will's hand! Maybe he'd been simply shaking hands with her – it was impossible to tell. But it was obvious that the guy wasn't letting go. At least, not anywhere fast enough for Matt's liking.

I can't believe it, Matt thought, his heart sinking. That must be the guy with the motorcycle.

He has that whole "I'm cool and I know it" thing going on.

As Matt drew closer, things got even worse. Will giggled and said to the guy, "So it's decided, Eric. You'll sit next to me!"

"You'll like it here!" Cornelia added. "You'll see."

"Isn't he the greatest?" Hay Lin said, as if she were the president of the guy's fan club or something.

Matt was disgusted. The girls were falling all over themselves to make the guy feel good, and Matt was dying to know what he'd done to deserve such treatment. Had he taken Will out to a better restaurant? Matt wondered bitterly. Had he sent her more messages than Matt had? And why was she sneaking around with some other guy before she'd even told Matt it was over between them?

All of Matt's high expectations for the first day of school evaporated on the spot. He would have done anything to slink away without speaking to her. But Will would spot him any second, and he couldn't let her know he was hurt. It would be awful if she knew the effect she had on him.

I'm more angry than hurt, anyway, he rationalised. I should have known this was going to happen.

Women, Matt thought, seething. They're all the same. But if Will wants it this way, fine. She can have the guy with the purple shirt – and she can count me out of her life! I don't need to be the runner-up. The second best. Last year's next new thing. I'll just have to toughen up. This'll teach me never to believe anything a girl says . . . again!

SEVEN

Will had never been so antsy in her life. She'd read about characters in books being ready to jump out of their skins – the image had always creeped her out. But now she could totally relate.

That's me! she thought. It could really happen if I have to wait another minute for Matt to show up.

The worst thing was that she didn't want to look too eager. She stood outside the school, trying hard to appear nonchalant and to speak in a nonchalant voice.

My friends must guess how much this is killing me, though, Will thought. That's why Cornelia tucked the tag in to the back of my shirt and Hay Lin said my hair looked great.

They're not fooled by my act. But will Matt be, though? He's got to know that I like him. But I can't let him know how much he's been on my mind since I last saw him. It's totally embarrassing!

Suddenly, Hay Lin cried, "There he is!" and started to gnaw on her fingernails. Will could feel the blood rush to her face, making her blush. Her friend must mean that Matt was heading their way! It was the moment she'd been waiting for all summer long.

But then she realised that Hay Lin was looking at somebody else, a boy that Will had never seen before. He was tall and gangly, with dark, wavy hair and friendly brown eyes. He hands were shoved into his pockets as he made his way towards Hay Lin. Will took note of his purple T-shirt. Hay Lin said he sort of marched to his own beat. That was a good thing in a guy, Will decided. Matt did that, too.

Before she could get back into Matt mode, the guy was bounding towards them, saying, "Hi, Hay Lin!" He didn't even wait to be introduced to the rest of the crowd – Hay Lin probably told him all about us, Will realised. "You must be Will," the boy said excitedly. "And

Taranee, Cornelia, and Irma," he continued down the line. "Nice to meet you!"

"Guys, this is Eric Lyndon," Hay Lin explained. Will thought that the only thing better than seeing Matt after all this time might be seeing Hay Lin with a crush – her happiness was contagious. She reached out her hand to shake Eric's. Something in his grip reassured Will – it was as if he wanted her to feel that he would treat Hay Lin right. Will shook his hand until Eric finally let go. She was totally impressed.

Then she felt Irma poke her. Leaning in towards Will's ear she whispered, "Hey, Will, look who's here!" Smiling, Irma moved her head in the direction of the gate, and pointed. Matt was right there, about to walk through. He hadn't spotted her yet, but he'd be by her side in about thirty seconds, as soon as he'd made his way through a crowd of kids.

Will drew in her breath and exhaled slowly. She didn't dare to check her hair again or anything like that, but she did take a moment to compose herself. Then she pretended to be engrossed in watching some other guys throw a Frisbee, secretly hoping nobody would guess how stressed she was.

I just hope he's thought about me half as much as I've thought about him! Will thought. That would be a nice way to start the school year!

When Matt approached, she turned towards him, ready to greet him with the perfect balance of caring and cool. Then Irma blew the moment by practically throwing herself at him and shrieking, "Ma-a-a-att! What a surprise!"

"Cut it out, Irma," Will muttered. Why had Irma picked a time like that to go into full-flirt mode – with her guy!

But Irma didn't seem to register with Matt at all. He glanced quickly in the girls' direction and said, "Hi, Irma, hi, Will." Then he marched right up to Eric as if he had some kind of problem with him. "Aren't you going to introduce me to your friend?" he grumbled in Will's direction.

Will seriously thought she was going to faint. What was Matt's problem? His attitude had completely blindsided her. She had no idea what was wrong.

Eric didn't seem to sense the hostility that was evident in Matt's tone. He just grinned.

"Hi," he said. "My name's Eric."

Hay Lin wrapped her arm around him and added awkwardly, "Um . . . yeah . . . right . . . Eric is in Will and Cornelia's class this year."

Hay Lin was definitely picking up on Matt's bad vibe and trying to calm things down.

So it's not just in my head, Will realised.

She wasn't sure if that was a good thing or a bad thing.

Matt didn't bother to introduce himself or return Eric's smile. He folded his arms, as if he were mad about something, and stared into space, looking right past Will.

Will bit her tongue as hard as she could and forced herself not to cry. She was blushing again, as if she had done something embarrassing.

But what could it be? she wondered. I haven't seen him in weeks! I'm innocent of all charges! What on earth is wrong? Was she supposed to say something now? she wondered. Since she couldn't, she didn't. But she glared at each of her friends in turn as if to say, "*You* say something." Nobody took the bait.

Nobody except Martin Tubbs. Martin was a nerdy guy who'd been crushing on Irma for ages. Once, she'd even gone on a sort of date with him. The two were definitely not an item, but they were friends in a way. Martin tutored Irma in French, and she put up with him in a manner that nobody else did. From the corner of her eye, Will could see Martin running up to them. He had a knack for always being in the wrong place at the wrong time.

"Hey, folks!" Martin exclaimed, in his usual clueless manner. "What's this, a funeral?"

Will was so upset about Matt that the sight of Martin was a welcome relief. Anything to change the subject, she thought. But Irma didn't feel the same way. She squinted at him and snapped, "Zip it, Martin!"

Martin sidled up a little closer to her. "Already missing vacation, Honey Muffin?" he asked sweetly. "But never fear, Martin's here! Nothing to worry about!" Will thought for a moment he was going to go ahead and give her a kiss. Eeek!

Irma rolled her eyes and pretended not to hear him. Anyone else would have taken the hint, but not Martin. He spotted Eric and kept on babbling. "Oh, a new kid on the block, I see!" he said with a mock bow. "I hope they gave you a proper welcome."

Eric shrugged modestly. "Oh, well . . ." he stammered.

Will didn't hear the rest of his reply, because suddenly Irma was stomping over to where Matt stood, his back to them all, sulking. "Enough is enough," she ordered. "You creep!"

She's just sticking up for me, Will told herself. That's what friends are supposed to do. But does she have to call him names? It's *Matt*! I liked him until about two seconds ago. She can't lose her temper with *him*! Will didn't want anybody sticking up for her just then – especially hotheaded Irma. She just wanted to run inside, hide in the bathroom, and pretend that none of this had ever happened.

"Ouch," said Matt sarcastically. He didn't look hurt at all.

Martin's eyes bugged out. "Irma, sweet thing!" he cooed. "What are you doing?"

Matt commiserated with Martin. "Yeah, what's got into her?" he asked, throwing up his hands.

What's got into *you*? Will wanted to retort. Instead she stood there staring at him, her eyes beginning to well up, until Irma grabbed her hand and hauled her away.

Scratch what I just said about not needing anyone to stick up for me, Will admitted to herself as the tears began to flow. I need somebody to get me out of here, quick!

Irma led her four friends around the corner of the building, stopping under the window of the principal's office. It was safe there. Nobody would gather in that spot unless they absolutely had to – like the five members of W.I.T.C.H.

Will was sobbing now, gasping for air as it all sank in. Somehow she had managed to mess everything up with Matt – and she didn't even know how! She was sort of mad at herself for blundering into some mistake she couldn't identify. But she was a lot madder at Matt.

And to think I wasted so much time mooning over him this summer, Will thought, wiping her nose. How could I have been so dumb? What did I ever see in him, anyway?

She would never forget, or forgive, the way he'd blown right past her, acting as if she weren't there. Or the way he'd mocked Irma, when she was just trying to help!

Taranee hugged her, hard, and Will kept asking, "Did you see that? He didn't even say hello to me!" as if Taranee would know why.

Her friend stroked Will's hair. "Maybe there's an explanation," she said consolingly.

There'd better be, Will thought, or else I'm going to have to switch schools. I can't spend this whole year feeling like some kind of reject!

"Just take it easy," Cornelia cautioned, not even knowing what dire thoughts were flying through Will's mind. "It's going to be OK. I just know it."

"Men," said Irma, sounding as if she bore the weight of the world on her shoulders. "Jeez!"

Will smiled wanly and remembered something terrible. No matter how awful she felt, she was going to have to walk into school soon. No way was Matt going to see her like that! Will resolved. She swallowed the rest of her tears and held a bottle of water she had grabbed from her book bag to her forehead. Maybe the cold would soothe the puffiness around her eyes. She would do whatever it took to keep her cool.

She looked at her friends' concerned faces and was filled with a wave of appreciation. What would I do without you? she asked them silently. How can I ever thank you? They'd dragged her away just as she was about to lose it, in public, on the first day of school. They'd saved her reputation at school – and her standing with Matt.

He might not like me any more, Will thought, but at least he won't see me as a pathetic loser. I *will* be strong when I walk into school! He will not see me cry!

She was about to say something corny but heartfelt to her best friends when there was a deafening noise.

Driiiiing!

"The bell!" said Hay Lin. "We have to go in now!"

"Aw, pipe down," said Irma, addressing herself more to the alarm than to Hay Lin. She never cared if she was a little late.

Then, with an earsplitting pop, the bell fell silent. Through her tears, Will grinned at her friends. It was a tradition at the Sheffield Institute to rig the bell to break down on the first day of school. Everyone knew that the principal and the custodian tried to stop this – but the kids always got around them.

Some things never change, thought Will.

Like the bell trick and the Power of Five. Boys may come and go, but friends like these will pull me through. Now . . . if only I can find my way to homeroom!

EIGHT

A world away, in another place, where no bell had been heard in centuries, the only sounds were the roar of the wind, the gushing of lava, and the occasional screams of the sole human inhabitant of the place, a prisoner.

A volcano lay at the heart of this wilderness, simmering and burbling, preparing to blow. It was surrounded by thick ice, utterly impassable, which had, over time, grown into massive formations that towered over the ground. Ice coated even the thinnest branch of the smallest tree in this desolate landscape. It also coated the heart of this remote kingdom's ruler: Nerissa.

It's hardly a kingdom, the ruler thought resentfully. It is a prison of ice that is as frozen and stale as my soul itself. It is quite a good fit.

Nerissa no longer knew feelings like contentment or pleasure. But she was not displeased at the moment, not at all. So far, everything had gone according to plan. Her servants Ember, Tridart, and Shagon had intercepted the Herald of Candracar at a seaside resort on earth. They had snatched him from the very arms of his beloved, the blonde Guardian, and placed him in Nerissa's hands! And they had also delivered some important news to Nerissa: she was not the only one in pursuit of the Herald's powers – exact copies of those held by the Guardians.

Nerissa remembered Luba well from her days as a Guardian. Even then, Luba had tended the Aurameres, observing them carefully as they spun around their chambers, alert for any evidence that the Guardians' magic was changing.

It is no wonder, Nerissa snorted to herself, that the cat-woman lost her mind. Her work was more tedious than my exile in Mount Thanos! But, of course, Nerissa would not allow Luba to carry out her plan. The powers would be hers!

Back in Riddlescott Lane, when she had spotted Luba, Ember had brought her down and branded her with the mark of Nerissa forever. It had been a great moment.

But Luba is not dead, Nerissa cautioned herself, so I must continue to keep an eye on her. Now, though, she knows that the Herald's powers are intended for my use alone! When she is brought back to Candracar, she will carry the first tangible evidence that I am advancing on their pristine Temple. And what I wouldn't give to see her sentenced for trying to use the Herald against the Oracle! They should thank me for stopping her in her tracks.

Nerissa rubbed her palms together in anticipation of what she was about to do next. Then she struggled to her feet and grabbed an icicle to support her weight.

I have to see the Herald again! she decided. I have to convince him to give me his set of powers. Of course, I could force the issue through torture, but it would be so much better if he would surrender of his own accord. I have to preserve every ounce of my strength! My precious magic must be spent only on my larger goal!

It was fitting that she, once a prisoner in this forgotten land, now had a prisoner of her own to torment. And when she'd finished having her fun with him, his powers would be hers! Naturally she would use them to get to the Guardians, to bring them down one by one, until at last she reclaimed the Heart of Candracar for herself.

Her dreams of that moment had sustained her for many long decades, and even just thinking of her reunion with the Heart made Nerissa's fingers quiver in anticipation. With every passing moment, she was one step closer to controlling the Heart. And with it, Nerissa exulted, she would control whatever else she pleased – including the Temple of Candracar itself!

As she moved slowly towards the place where the captive lay, Nerissa could hear his guards moving about. *Aaaaaaargh!* was the hateful cry of Shagon. And *Ahhhhuuuu!* was the howl of Khor, the creature she had formed from the little dog that had wandered mistakenly towards Mount Thanos.

When she was close to Caleb's molten prison, Nerissa could also hear his piteous cry.

"They can't do this to me!" she heard him groan.

He is afraid, Nerissa thought with a smile. As well he should be.

His moaning only stopped when Nerissa stood directly before him. She vaguely recalled what it was like to welcome someone, to try to make them feel at home. She drew on that distant memory and asked her servants archly, "How is our guest today? I hope he is not feeling too neglected."

The boy did not return her show of good manners. He closed his eyes as if to shut her out. Nerissa could barely conceal her glee. "We prepared such a warm welcome for you, Caleb," she continued. "The least you could do is show a little gratitude!"

He remained silent until Nerissa grew angry.

How dare he ignore me? she raged inwardly. His only option is to please me. "Don't you have anything to say to me?" she urged him at last. She glared at Caleb until he finally opened his eyes.

"Yes," he whispered. "I'm thirsty!"

Nerissa doubled over with laughter and turned to her servants. "Did you hear that?"

she asked them bitterly. "Our little Caleb is thirsty!"

Bending courteously in her direction, Tridart smirked. "I want to make you happy, my friend!" he said sarcastically to Caleb. Nerissa had formed him from the ice that surrounded her volcanic home. He was definitely the man – or thing – for this job.

Nerissa's servant half turned away from Caleb and drew up his feathered wings. When he flexed them, a chunk of ice flew off the edge of one of them and right into Caleb's cell.

"After all, you can't refuse a doomed man his last request," Nerissa said scornfully as she watched Caleb leap out of the way of the flying ice.

Caleb was livelier than he'd been since she'd trapped him. "Think you're funny, do you?" he rasped.

"I'm just trying to be kind, Caleb!" Nerissa insisted, not bothering to try and hide the sarcasm growing in her voice. "That chunk of ice will be all the water you get! Go ahead and drink it!"

My hospitality is fading fast, she chuckled

to herself. Believe me, when I decide to make my move, you won't stay strong for long. You will be begging for more than water – you'll be begging for your life!

NINE

The Oracle had often turned to his reflecting pool to check on the welfare of his Guardians down on the earth. With one glance into the pool's shimmering waters, the Oracle could see any place in the universe. Now he was anxious to observe how the Herald fared with Nerissa.

Sighing heavily, he waited for the image to come into focus. It was not long ago that he had witnessed a scene of triumph reflected there, as his handpicked Guardians had closed the portals and saved Meridian. The Oracle smiled as he remembered the pride he'd felt as they'd mastered their magic and taken it into Metamoor.

It had been amazing to watch each girl's transformation. As they grew more confident in their powers, they grew more confident in themselves.

Quiet and shy Taranee had learned to let out her fiery side and face challenges head on. Cornelia, always one to lead, had quickly learned the value of following. And Irma, the wild and unpredictable one of the group, had become a solid and reliable member. Hay Lin had also come into her own, following in her grandmother's footsteps. And perhaps Will had come the furthest, taking on and embracing the challenges that came with being the leader.

But it seemed a long time now since everything had gone according to the Oracle's wishes. When Cornelia had broken away from her friends to care for Caleb, the Guardians' path had become less steady. The group that had grown together suddenly seemed impossibly broken. And the Oracle's plans had been truly shattered when Luba interfered with the fate of the girls.

The Oracle shook his head in wonder. What could I have done to stop Luba? he wondered. Could I have done anything differently?

Much had changed since then – it was hard to fathom. His brow furrowed suddenly as the full horror of the scene that was unfolding near Mount Thanos came into view. It was terrible to see the agony on Caleb's face – quite a different sight from the one in which the boy had triumphed in Meridian.

In every life, the Oracle knew, some rain must fall. But perhaps this storm was too much for the Herald to bear. After all, he has already been through so much.

It is almost too much for *me* to bear, the Oracle admitted silently. But there is no other way. Our only hope is for events to unfold exactly as I have planned.

Over the many millennia, the Oracle had stuck by countless difficult and unpopular decisions. But this one seemed more dreadful, somehow, than the others. The image of the suffering Caleb brought the Oracle great sorrow.

Under his breath, he encouraged the boy. "Be strong, Caleb!" the Oracle urged him. "The one who can help you is not yet ready! It will take days . . . perhaps weeks . . ."

In truth, there was no exact time frame, but the Oracle knew that help would eventually come. Caleb just had to hang on for a little while longer. If he could . . .

Beside him, suddenly, the Oracle could hear soft footseps. He did not want to be interrupted at that moment, not even by his trusted friend, Yan Lin. But here she was, her arms crossed and a frown etched among the deep lines of her face. She did not even have to speak for the Oracle to know her displeasure, but nevertheless, she did.

"What are we waiting for?" she cried. She had also had a glimpse of Caleb's ordeal at the hands of Nerissa, and could not understand the Oracle's hesitation.

It was the very question that was plaguing the Oracle, the very question for which he had no answer. His voice strained as he answered. "We've already discussed this, Yan Lin," the Oracle replied.

"But this is madness!" she insisted. "There is nothing good that can come of such a decision."

The Oracle held up a hand to interrupt her. "And you know perfectly well what I have decided."

Her face fell, and she lowered her eyes. She did not budge, so the Oracle could tell she was not done confronting him. "Are you questioning my position?" he asked her slowly. That would go against all of the peaceful and orderly traditions of Candracar.

Yan Lin wrung her hands anxiously. It was clear to the Oracle that the situation was upsetting her greatly. The two of them had rarely disagreed. "Pardon my insolence, Oracle! I'm afraid that your trust has been poorly rewarded."

It was not exactly an apology, but Yan Lin acknowledged that she'd been out of line. The Oracle had the capacity for infinite forgiveness – and he had a soft spot for Yan Lin. He was not angry with her then, but he sorely wished he could bring her around to his point of view.

I am going to need every one of the Elders firmly beside me as we battle Nerissa and her dark forces, he thought. And as we put our faith in the hands of such a young Herald . . . and Guardians.

He would need to let Yan Lin know she was still in his favour. So the Oracle led her up a glittering staircase to yet another aerie, with yet another splendid view of the Temple. He gazed out over Candracar as if to say, "Here it is: all we have to preserve; all that is at stake in the coming fight." Then he turned to Yan Lin. "The person has been chosen," he said. "It is no longer the time to discuss this matter. We must accept what is to be. There is no other option."

With any luck, Yan Lin would cease to interrogate him. With any luck, she would respect his wishes for just a bit longer. He only hoped there was time for his plan to work.

TEN

The first day of school was finally over. And it couldn't have come soon enough, Taranee thought. Now, classes could be forgotten, and more important things could be handled.

Taranee hurried to Will's house a few minutes behind her friends. She'd parted ways with the other girls just a few blocks from school with a special mission in mind. There was only one thing she could think of to brighten up that dreary afternoon: a box of candy. So she had stopped at a fancy shop around the corner from Sheffield Institute. She'd selected a few dozen chocolates and watched as they were packed in a big blue box with three layers. No gloppy fillings here – and no nuts! thought Taranee with satisfaction. Just pure, smooth chocolate.

Guaranteed to mend a broken heart . . . or at least satisfy a sweet tooth.

Making her way through downtown Heatherfield, Taranee passed the Lodelyday, the place where Matt and Will had had the first part of their first date. Until Matt forgot his wallet, Taranee remembered with a smile. Luckily it was an awkward moment that turned out OK!

Who would ever have guessed things would end up like this? Taranee thought sadly. Who would have thought they'd end up fighting on the first day of school. They seemed like the perfect couple!

She still remembered her first impression of Matt, back when she was new in town. He seemed cool and unapproachable, with his long hair and his carefully sloppy clothes. He was totally crushworthy. And that was *before* she'd found out he was the guitarist in a band so good that they had once opened at a Karmilla concert! Talk about a dream guy.

But Taranee quickly discovered that Matt wasn't all rock 'n' roll. She had come to see a different side of him through Will. Matt didn't spend his free time cultivating his rock-star image or anything like that – instead, he worked at his uncle's pet shop. He had a quiet sense of humour and a sweet way with words. Will had let her friends read all the messages Matt sent her while they were at Irma's, and Taranee couldn't help wishing that someone – like Nigel, maybe – would write messages like that to her! Everything seemed so right between them, mused Taranee. So how had it gone so wrong . . . so quickly?

Taranee was the bookish one in the group, and from all her reading she *knew* there had to be an explanation for Matt's odd behaviour. But nobody is going to try and figure it *all* out right now, Taranee told herself as she walked into Will's building.

It wasn't like her to put off a problem for later – Taranee liked to delve right in and analyse things from every angle. Dissect the problems and create solutions. Today, however, that wasn't the point. She and her friends had to be there for Will, pure and simple. There would be time after the chocolate . . . and some crying, to deal with Matt.

She rode the elevator up to Will's floor and let herself in to the apartment. Inside, she was greeted by silence. Taranee made her way through the apartment and found her friends sprawled on Will's couch while Will paced back and forth. Taranee cocked an eyebrow at Hay Lin as if to ask, "What's going on?" Hay Lin just shrugged in response. They were following Will's lead, apparently, and Will wasn't talking. So neither were they.

Quietly, Taranee put the box of chocolates on the coffee table. Still eerily quiet, her friends pounced on them like a pack of starving wolves. Taranee joined in. She ate one piece, and then another, her mind drifting back to the earlier scene at school.

So much had happened that morning that she hadn't really had the chance to think about meeting Hay Lin's new crush, Eric. He had seemed nice, Taranee decided as she crinkled up a chocolate wrapper. Nice was always a good quality in a boy. And it seemed as though he genuinely wanted to get to know them, which was a good sign.

He gets the big thumbs-up, she thought. So I guess that means that all five of us have a crush now. Who would have thought we'd all pair up . . . or at least have the potential to pair up? Maybe someday we'll go on a quintuple date!

The thought almost made her laugh out loud. She caught herself just in time. When she had gotten herself under control, she reviewed all of the couples in her mind. There were Hay Lin and Eric, who were still getting to know each other, and Will and Matt – it was too soon to write them off. Taranee knew she shouldn't count Martin as Irma's crush, but sometimes she wondered . . . and Martin definitely had a crush on Irma. Plus, Irma always had a crush of the moment, so she would always be up for a date. And Taranee? Well, Taranee had been crushing on Nigel for a long time now. She was hoping, though, she'd see more of him this year – maybe even persuade her mum to like him.

Once, he'd got in trouble for trespassing at the Heatherfield Museum, and Taranee's mum had just happened to be the judge who sentenced him to some long hours of community service. Nigel didn't seem to hold it against Taranee, but her mum always thought Nigel was in with the wrong crowd, no matter how much he changed. Sometimes Taranee felt as though she were in the middle of a lose-lose battle.

Her eyes fell on a newsmagazine that Will's

mum had left next to the couch. Would it be too rude if I picked it up and started reading? she wondered.

Taranee was suddenly filled with the weirdest feeling. She felt as though she were failing to remember something important that had happened over the summer. What was it? She could picture Irma's beach house, and the place she'd gone later with her own family, the mountain village of Sesamo, but there was something missing. Taranee tried to think what she was forgetting; she couldn't shake the feeling that something else big had happened over the summer. She was about to reach for the magazine, hoping to jog her memory a little, when Irma started muttering something with her mouth full.

"One . . . two . . . shree . . ." Taranee tried to tune it out, but Irma kept on going. "Five . . . shix . . ." Irma took another bite. "Sheven . . . eight . . ."

"Cut it out, Irma!" Cornelia interrupted. She wasn't known for her patience . . . especially when it came to anything Irma did or said. The two of them didn't exactly see eye to eye.

"What's your problem?" Irma demanded,

giving Cornelia an angry look before she explained. "Will's pacing, and I'm keeping count."

Nobody responded, because suddenly Will spoke. She'd stopped moving as she froze in front of the window. Will leaned against it, her arms crossed above her head, and started saying, "You're so dumb, You're so dumb," aloud, but obviously to herself. She seemed completely unaware of the worried girls nearby.

It was a terrible thing for her friends to hear. "Don't be so hard on yourself," said Taranee gently. Will was their leader; she couldn't break down now – especially not over a boy! She had faced so many things that had seemed so much worse.

Cornelia seemed to agree. "You need to let it all out, Will. But Taranee's right – it isn't your fault!" Then, with no warning whatsoever, Cornelia ran over and got Irma in a mock head-lock. With a grin she added, "You know, Will, you could always pick on Irma. It might make you feel a little better. I have to admit, it makes *me* feel better. If I were you, I would have done it by now myself!" But Cornelia looked pretty serious, and Taranee wondered if she should do something.

Irma kept squirming, but Cornelia had pinned her. "Stop it!" Irma cried. "I'm not kidding, Corny! Knock it off!"

I wish they'd leave each other alone, Taranee thought. Why are they acting like this right now?

She knew the answer. It's because we don't know what else to do, she decided. None of us has ever been hurt this much by a boy. So, we are doing our best – but I'm not sure that's enough.

Taranee's worries were interrupted by Hay Lin, who approached her and glanced at the couch where Cornelia and Irma were still wrestling.

"Want me to make some tea?" Hay Lin asked. It was what she always did when people were feeling blue.

Taranee nodded – she sure didn't have any better ideas.

Will's head whipped around when she heard Hay Lin's offer. Hay Lin looked at her reassuringly and added, "It's my special tea! You know . . . the one that even helps you stomach boys' stupidity!" Hay Lin turned and walked into the kitchen.

Somehow the words got through to Will. She turned away from the window and grabbed a tissue, blew her nose, rubbed her eyes, and stared at the floor. "I was really hoping that Matt and I . . ." she began, her voice a little calmer.

Don't even say it, thought Taranee. "I'm sure there's a reason for what he did," she interjected in a rush. "He's not that kind of guy. . . ."

All of a sudden Will was crying again. "I hate him!" she blubbered. "Yeah, I hate him!"

They all knew that that was *so* not true . . . Will knew it herself. She burst into yet another crying fit.

Taranee joined Cornelia and Irma on the couch, and all three of them turned to peer over the back of it at Will.

For a moment, Taranee wondered if in fact Will wanted *not* to talk.

Taranee was quiet, sometimes, and definitely a private person. She hated it when she shared her feelings with her friends, only to regret having done so later. It made her feel guilty . . . and even more alone. Even though Taranee knew her friends would always listen, she still kept a lot to herself. Maybe Will was feeling the same way.

I'm changing, though, Taranee reminded herself. It wasn't long ago that I was a total fraidycat, wary of new situations, and super shy. Back then I would *never* share – not even if it made me feel ten times better. But that's not me any more.

She thought about all the brave things she'd done with her Guardian friends, the bad guys they had faced and the various people they had saved. That part of her wanted to tell Will to pick up her phone and demand an explanation from Matt. But the other part wasn't sure she would have followed her own advice!

Things were so much less complicated this past summer, Taranee sighed. There hadn't been any boys at Irma's house that week when they were at the beach, and it had been perfect. It had been fun to talk about boys, and call them, and tease one another about them. But it was a lot more peaceful with the boys at a distance!

Taranee watched as Will walked around the sofa and finally threw herself at her friends' feet. She leaned her elbows on Cornelia's lap and asked them all, "How can you guys even put up with me?"

Hay Lin came back into the room carrying a tray with five steaming cups of tea, just in time to lighten the mood. "We *put up* with Irma," she quipped, "but *you*, we're crazy about." Her tone was just right, enough to bring a wry smile to Will's face.

"Hey!" complained Irma, feeling the brunt of one too many jokes at her expense. Taranee could tell Irma had had enough.

Cornelia smiled smugly. "Well said, Hay Lin."

Just then, Taranee remembered something. She dug in the back pocket of her jeans for a handkerchief she'd carried with her for good luck on the first day of school. It was a little old-fashioned, she knew – who used a hand-kerchief these days? But her grandmother had given it to her, so it always felt special to Taranee. Plus, it went with the romantic off-the-shoulder shirt she'd chosen to wear that day! She'd been so caught up with Will and Matt that she had had no idea if Nigel had noticed it. Taranee had a lot more to offer than a stylish back-to-school wardrobe, though.

The handkerchief was a source of strength, totally apart from W.I.T.C.H.: a reminder of who she was and where she came from. She needed all the reminding she could get these days! But someone else needed a handkerchief a lot more than she did. "Come on, Will!" she said, handing it over. "No more tears, OK?"

ELEVEN

Eric Lyndon followed Martin Tubbs down the steps of the main building at Sheffield Institute. He was utterly and thoroughly exhausted. It had been a long day of learning names, smiling at everyone he met, and trying not to get lost. He didn't exactly miss his old school – his family had moved around a lot, so he never got too attached to one place – but he *definitely* missed the feeling of fitting in.

Sometimes I get sick of finding my way around a new place over and over again, he admitted to himself. After one too many times, the appeal of being the new kid again wears off . . . big-time. It would be nice to start a new year in the same place where I spent the last one!

One thing that made the day a little easier, though, Eric thought, was seeing Hay Lin. And her friends were pretty cool, too.

Hay Lin had already told him all about them during the summer, but meeting them in person gave him a much better picture. He could tell immediately that the five friends were a tight-knit group. Irma seemed every bit as bubbly as Hay Lin had described her, while Taranee was studious but sweet. Even Cornelia, the "popular" one of the group, was just what he had expected – beautiful but completely approachable. The only person he couldn't quite find a connection with was Will. It had seemed as if something were bugging her, Eric thought, recalling the meeting. Something to do with that guy Matt, maybe?

A girl in his old school had once told Eric that he was good at figuring people out. She had called him intuitive. Eric would never have described himself that way, but he had to admit that it was true that he could tell things about people's characteristics before he really got to know them. It was as if he picked up on their vibe or something. He could tell almost instantly if they were "good" people. That was why he'd liked Hay Lin the instant he'd almost hit her with his motorbike. That was also why he'd sensed Will's discomfort that morning. And right now, he had a feeling about this Martin Tubbs, too. Eric didn't want to give himself too much credit – the kid's uniform was kind of a giveaway – but Eric was willing to bet that Martin wasn't exactly your average Sheffield student. He was nice and outgoing, but a little strange. Martin was definitely eccentric, and Eric liked that about him. After meeting so many people that all seemed the same – despite the school – Martin's quirky personality was refreshing.

And being eccentric definitely didn't seem to bother Martin. He was just eager to help – anybody. It turned out that Martin lived in Eric's new neighbourhood, and so as soon as Eric mentioned that fact, he'd volunteered to teach Eric a shortcut home – showing him some local sights along the way.

So now he found himself following Martin as he briskly led the way across a busy street. Then Martin piped up with the same question Eric had been asked, oh, a hundred times that day. "So, where did you live before coming here?"

"I lived in Scandinavia for a couple of months," Eric explained patiently. "My folks were working on a space research project." He figured that space exploration was right up Martin's alley and would keep him preoccupied enough to prevent more "where are you from" questions.

Sure enough, Martin did a double take when he heard the words "space" and "station." "Really?" he gushed. "The Happy Bears will be crazy about your stories! Want to come to today's meeting with me?"

Well, that explains the outfit, Eric thought with a smile. But he had never heard of the Happy Bears. It was yet another one of the annoying things about always being a fish out of water – he never knew the ins and outs of any school . . . or its groups. Were the Happy Bears a Heatherfield group – in which case nobody would expect him to know about them – or a group with members everywhere, which he'd just happened to miss hearing about? Eric got the sense he shouldn't ask too many questions if he didn't want to join. Martin seemed a bit too eager to sign him up and slap a uniform on him. He'd have to stick with a light and witty response. "I'll only come if I can have a uniform just like yours!" he said.

"Nice, isn't it?" asked Martin without a trace of irony, touching the bandanna tied neatly around his neck. "You have no idea what effect it has on girls!"

Suddenly, Eric realised he'd got another vibe from Martin, one that seemed so outlandish it hadn't even registered at first. Maybe Martin had been lingering on the fringes of Hay Lin's crowd for a reason . . . or for some*one*. "Girls?" he repeated. "Like Irma?" Eric didn't have to wait long to find out if his guess was right.

Martin blushed a deep shade of purple. "Well, Irma's used to uniforms. Her father's a policeman," he said. "With her, I just use my captivating charm. No need to rely on the uniform."

Turning his back to Martin for a second, Eric broke into a huge grin. He couldn't wait to tell Hay Lin what Martin had said. She would get a total kick out of Martin's confession. Eric composed himself quickly and glanced at his watch to see how much time he had to kill before he could call Hay Lin's house. Even though he had seen her during the day, he was already missing her voice. But by now he knew not to call before the dinner rush was over at the restaurant. He sighed – there was still a lot of time left.

He walked faster and caught up again with Martin, who had not stopped walking. He couldn't afford to lose the guy; he had no idea where he was! Besides, he had nothing else to do, and Martin seemed intent on showing him around.

The boys approached a long flight of stairs that led to a pedestrian bridge that spanned the street. They climbed the stairs and walked onto the bridge. Martin was momentarily quiet, so Eric had a chance to take in the scenery. The downtown area quickly gave way to quiet residential streets, with fenced-in green yards and cars in the driveways. Every once in a while a large building would appear, but for the most part, it was picture-perfect. In fact, it was all so bright and shiny that it almost made Eric's eyes hurt. Heatherfield was a long way from the frozen wasteland where he'd spent the past several months with his family.

It's hard to imagine feeling at home here,

thought Eric. I haven't lived in a city in a long time. It feels like I have been isolated. On the other hand, though, there are people like Hay Lin and her friends here. So maybe it won't be that bad.

Eric's thoughts were shattered by Martin, who got another burst of energy and launched back into his "how to woo girls" monologue. It was as if there hadn't just been several minutes of silence between them.

"I'll teach you how it's done, if you want," Martin offered. He was looking hopefully at Eric, waiting for a response.

Eric figured he'd play along and see where this led. "Aren't you worried about competition?" he asked Martin.

"Na-a-a-ah!" said Martin. "I can see you're a guy I can trust." Then he abruptly switched topics, as if he had changed his mind and wasn't sure he should talk about the topic any more. "Are you coming to the fireworks show?" he asked.

Does he think Irma will be by his side? Eric asked himself. Well, maybe Hay Lin will be by mine! He was still glowing with the memory of the night of the shooting stars he had shared with Hay Lin. And fireworks were *almost* as romantic. "Hey, why not?" he said noncommittally. "When are they?"

"Day after tomorrow," Martin replied. "And if Irma stops beating up the guitarist, Cobalt Blue is going to play." He blushed again when he said her name.

Eric quickly put two and two together. Irma had almost beat up that guy Matt, the one who seemed to have upset Will. "Cobalt Blue," he said. "Is that your friend's band?" It might have been a stretch to call Matt and Martin friends (they were *so* different), but Eric didn't know how else to describe him.

"Yep," Martin confirmed. Proudly, he added, "They're pretty good. They were the opening act at the Karmilla concert!"

Karmilla's reputation had travelled even to the remotest corners of world – Eric was impressed. "So, Matt's band opened for Karmilla? Wow!" Hay Lin had neglected to tell him that her friend had a crush on a budding rock star. He could see how that might make things complicated – and how it might account for Will's strange behaviour.

Martin's voice dropped as he confided

something to Eric. "I have a feeling something happened between Matt and Will," he said. "I pick up on things like that!"

Eric had to smile. So maybe he wasn't the only intuitive boy at the Sheffield Institute. It was good to know that he and Martin actually had something in common. From experience, Eric knew not to rule anybody out too quickly. You never knew who your friends were going to be. Still, he hoped that he would meet some guys that he had a little more in common with. But he'd have to deal with that at another point. Right now he needed to pay attention to this so-called shortcut.

He and Martin trudged past a stretch of stores and then through a city park. Just when he was wondering how that route could be termed a shortcut, a basketball appeared out of nowhere with a *Thud*! "What the . . .?" Eric asked. Moving quickly, he caught it on the first bounce.

"Hey, heads up!" someone called out from the basketball court in the park.

"Got it!" cried Eric. Could it be a little pick-up game? He hadn't gotten a chance to play basketball in a while and he was anxious to get onto the court. This would be the second-best thing that had happened to him since he had arrived in Heatherfield, the first having been the encounter with Hay Lin, of course.

A guy poked his head out from around the fence that separated the court from the park's walkway. He was tall, with straight, chin-length hair, and Eric could have sworn Hay Lin had pointed him out earlier. He was pretty sure the guy's name was Nigel. And one of Hay Lin's friends liked him – Taranee, he remembered. What a coincidence! Since the girls were friends, Nigel would be a good person to get to know. And, if the girls liked him, maybe Eric would, too.

"Martin! Good thing your friend caught the ball!" Nigel called, his eyes darting in Eric's direction. "It would've been the third one we lost today!" Martin giggled nervously, like someone who didn't know what to say in the presence of a piece of sports equipment.

"Feel like shooting a few hoops?" Nigel asked Eric and Martin with a friendly smile as the other boys on the court drew closer.

Eric was dying to jump right in – his own basketball was still packed in a box somewhere, and he hadn't played since his family's move. The game was one of his all-time favourites, and, since he was so tall, he wasn't half bad at it, either.

"What do you say?" Eric asked, turning to look at Martin.

Martin's response was just as he'd suspected. "Didn't you want to visit the city's historical sights?" he whined.

Nigel dribbled the ball as he waited for an answer. Eric weighed the different options. He felt bad ditching Martin, who was only trying to be nice, but Nigel's offer was too good to pass up. It usually took a lot longer than that for Eric to meet kids he thought he could really like . . . and he was eager to get back on the court.

"You don't mind, do you, Martin?" Eric asked awkwardly. It was painful to give Martin the brush-off after Martin had offered to be his tour guide, but he'd make it up to him some-how, make a special appearance at the Happy Bears or something. And he could always take the long way home.

Folding his arms, Martin muttered, "Culture always loses out to brute force!"

Eric caught Nigel's eye and saw in his

glance a confirmation of everything he had thought. Martin was nice, but a little strange, while Nigel was just the kind of guy that Eric needed to meet if he were ever to feel at home in Heatherfield. But Eric was saved from making any more decisions.

Diplomatically, Nigel said, "You can show him around later, Martin." Then he tossed the basketball to Eric and added, "Now it's time for us to play!"

TWELVE

He'll never find his way home without me, thought Martin smugly. And he'll never get to know *this town* if I don't show him around.

There was nothing Martin liked less than an uninformed citizen of Heatherfield – and nothing he liked more than recruiting new members for the Happy Bears. Eric would make a great addition to the Bears – he couldn't let him get away. Plus, Eric seemed like a really nice guy, and it would be fun to have a new friend.

It looked as if Martin were just going to have to stick around while the new guy played basketball. That way, he could continue his conversation with Eric Lyndon later.

I think he liked the idea, Martin thought confidently. Pretty soon he'll be coming to meetings twice a month!

Since Martin disdained any physical activity, he thought he might as well start his homework while the other boys ran around the court. It was never too early to get a head start on the new school year – Martin had read half of his textbooks over the summer already. But when he glanced up, things looked tense. Maybe watching *would* be more entertaining than reading.

Eric Lyndon dribbled the ball down the court. He looked like a natural ballplayer. "Look who's here!" Eric cried in surprise, when he almost barreled into another player.

Nigel filled in the name for him when he saw Eric looking quizzically at the player. "This is Matt!" he said. "And I'm Nigel, by the way – it's nice to meet you."

It was hard for Martin to believe the three of them hadn't met already, since they seemed alike in so many ways. And in Martin's experience, people who seemed alike usually ended up hanging out.

Martin's eyes bounced from Nigel to Eric to Matt like a Ping-Pong ball (that was one of the few sports he could stomach). Nigel looked genuinely pleased to meet Eric. But Matt was a different story altogether. He didn't look at all happy to see Eric Lyndon, and Martin was pretty sure he knew the reason why. Before he could say anything, Nigel spoke up.

"First one to ten wins!" he called, unaware of the tension on the court.

As the boys raced after the ball, Martin tried to reconstruct in his mind what had happened that morning. He knew that that had had something to do with Matt's evil looks at Eric.

Martin made it his business to learn everything he could about Irma and her crowd of friends. And the way he figured it, Will had a big crush on Matt. Martin had even spotted them one night, dressed up and heading together to the Lodelyday! It looked a lot like love.

But maybe it's no longer love, Martin thought. Will had been away for the end of the summer. So Will and Matt couldn't have seen each other in at least a few weeks, Martin surmised. They had probably been pretty psyched to see each other again – until Eric Lyndon had happened on the scene, that is.

Martin was proud of himself for putting it all together. Not that it had been hard to do. He considered himself quite the mystery solver.

He'd been heading towards Irma at the very moment when Will and Matt had reunited, and he'd happened to catch the looks on both their faces. Will had looked ecstatic, Martin remembered. But Matt had looked heartbroken . . . and angry.

And why was that? thought Martin. He was willing to bet it was because Will had just finished shaking Eric's hand. Unfortunately for Matt, Will hadn't seemed eager to let go of that hand.

Martin glanced over at Matt on the court. With his brooding eyes and goatee, the guy did look pretty intense. It wasn't hard to imagine that he might be the jealous type. He must, Martin thought, have thought that Will was *holding* Eric's hand, not shaking it. It was a simple mistake to make. If one were prone to overreacting. I'd never treat my Irma that way, thought Martin. I know she likes me – even if she ignores me.

But that still left one question, Martin thought. What was Eric Lyndon doing with that group of girls in the first place? It seemed as if he knew them pretty well already – or some of them, anyway. Martin hadn't yet put together that piece of the puzzle, but he knew he would, eventually.

My brain is like a well-oiled machine! he gloated. I never forget a detail, and I never fail to make connections.

The other boys were talking to each other over the sound of the basketball hitting the pavement. "So, Martin tells me you have a band," Eric said to Matt.

Look at Eric being all friendly to Matt, Martin thought. Too bad he has no clue that Matt has it in for him.

Matt was not interested in cheery chitchat. "Uh-huh . . ." he grunted in reply to Eric's question.

Eric probably just thinks Matt's engrossed in the game, Martin decided. But I know better. This game is headed for trouble.

Oblivious to Matt's irritation, Eric continued to talk to him. "Who knows? Maybe one day we could jam together," he said. "It could be fun."

"Hmph," said Matt, dismissing him. "We'll see." He tossed the ball through a basket to score a point – and, perhaps, to *make* a point.

Matt was in the lead now, and clearly happy to keep it that way.

Martin felt a little sorry for Eric. The guy needed some major saving. Martin to the rescue! "So you're a musician, Eric?" he asked from his spot on the side of the court. It wasn't every day that someone proposed a jam session with the guitarist from Cobalt Blue – he had better be good!

"I learned when I was little, from my grandpa," Eric said, stealing the ball from Matt and rushing in the other direction. "But I'm not too shabby at basketball, either." From halfway down the court, Eric went for the basket – and scored! Even Martin knew it was an impressive shot, and he could hear Matt whistle softly in grudging appreciation.

Eric acted as if it were no big deal. "Down at the observatory," he continued, running backwards, "there's a room full of musical instruments. I used to hide down there, and, boy, would my grandpa get mad!"

Matt rolled his eyes at Nigel when he thought that nobody was watching. But Martin saw.

I miss nothing, Martin congratulated himself.

What is Matt so annoyed by, anyway? Does he think that putting a ball through a hoop should come before a perfectly decent conversation?

Martin, for one, was a lot more interested in hearing Eric's reminiscences of childhood than he was in the game – even if Matt looked bored.

The *Tump! Tump!* of the bouncing ball almost drowned out Eric's voice, but Martin heard him finish with, " . . . Until one day my grandpa told me, 'Seeing as you like those things so much, why don't you choose one and train it?'"

What? Martin thought. Doesn't he know you train yourself to play an instrument – not the other way around?

Nigel was with him on that one. "Train an instrument?" he asked, confused. "How are you supposed to do that?"

"Yeah, I know. Kinda weird, huh?" said Eric. "Train an instrument. Teach it to do what you want it to. To play the kind of music you like . . ." His voice trailed off as he realised that nobody was quite following what he was saying. The guys looked pretty confused.

Martin was ready to lend him a hand again – after all, his ulterior motive was never too far from his mind. He saw real potential for Eric to be a Happy Bear! He could help them come up with a group song. Maybe Eric just needed a chance to explain, so he asked, "And then?"

But Matt blew him off. "Stay tuned for the next episode," he said, acting as if Eric's story were too long to care. "So, Eric," he changed the subject. "Are you leaving soon?"

Please! thought Martin. I've had enough of this game. He was more than ready to hit the road before somebody got hurt.

Eric, though, seemed to think Matt was asking him when he was leaving *town*. "I don't know. But I think I'll be here for a little while, at least. Heatherfield is full of great people," he said optimistically.

"You talking about Will?" Matt countered, his eyes narrowing.

Martin drew in his breath as Eric stammered to respond, "Well . . . her, too. But to tell you the truth, I was thinking of someone else." A moment passed, and then Eric added one more thing, just to clarify. "Plus, I get the feeling that Will has a real weakness for guitarists!"

Good save, Eric, Martin thought. Eric must have sensed that something was up between

Matt and Will, he guessed. Some people just knew those things.

The sour look on Matt's face sweetened up as he realised what Eric had just said. If Eric wasn't after Will, then Matt had nothing to worry about.

Except that he's wrong, he made a big mistake today, Martin thought. I saw Will crying with her friends. I bet it had something to do with Matt's cold behaviour.

Martin had no reason to dislike Matt, but he felt a loyalty to any friend of Irma's. After all, Martin was like an honorary member of her group, and any insult to Will was an insult to Irma – and an insult to him!

I feel Will's pain, Martin thought. Matt will need to make amends.

Martin had never thought Eric liked Will, anyway – he'd thought it was a mix-up from the start. Still, he didn't know why Eric had been with the girls that morning. . . . All at once, Eric proposed a new destination. "You guys feel like going to get something to eat at the Silver Dragon?" he asked.

Martin leaped up in the air triumphantly. At last the mystery had been solved. "Aha!" he cried. "Hay Lin!" Eric must have met her over the summer – and he probably had gone to her family's restaurant, too. That would explain Hay Lin's nervous look right before Eric had walked up to the group. It would also explain why Eric seemed to know the girls even before the school year had started.

Doing some quick calculation, Martin realised that there were five girls in Irma's inner circle, and four boys on the basketball court. They all matched up. Matt and Will. Eric and Hay Lin. Nigel and Taranee. And Irma and Martin! Well, *kind of*, Martin and Irma.

Martin knew they weren't exactly a couple, but he would never give up hope. Maybe one day he'd really be with her. Maybe one day he'd really be a part of that crowd.

The only girl missing, Martin realised, was Cornelia. People thought she was pretty. And popular. So why wasn't she dating anyone? Why hadn't her friends helped her out in the love department? It was a question Martin had never really considered before, and he decided to look into it. Maybe he would even find a solution, come to think of it.

I know, Martin said to himself, raising a finger in the air before he followed the other boys, who were heading to the restaurant. Maybe she needs to meet a Happy Bear!

THIRTEEN

Far inside Mount Thanos, Nerissa held her head in her hands. Flames danced around her, and lava burbled beneath her, but nothing was hotter or more fiery than the burning in Nerissa's heart.

The time has come, she realised. I cannot – *I must not* – wait any longer! I need to act now, before it is too late.

She had tried to work with the captive, to make him do her bidding without brute force. She'd hoped to find a kindred spirit buried within him – after all, she knew he had once served the dark and evil Prince Phobos. But Caleb had been influenced by the spirit of Candracar, with its lofty notions of loyalty and peace. She had

126

not been able to coerce him to her side. So now, Nerissa would resort to her back-up plan. She would take the powers from him with her own might . . . no matter what the cost to the boy.

For centuries, the only emotion Nerissa had felt was rage. It had filled her lonely tomb, as volatile as gas and ready to explode, crowding all fear and all pain out of her mind. Anger fueled her spirit and consumed her every thought.

Now, however, she was a bit worried about whether she could channel her anger in just the way she had planned. She intended to seize Caleb's copies of the Guardians' powers. With them in her control, she would transform herself into the ravishing young Guardian she once had been! She would be unbeatable.

From somewhere on earth, she could feel the Heart of Candracar calling her, begging her to rescue it from the impostor, Will. The young girl should not hold the Heart. Nerissa knew that the Heart was hers and always would be.

I will suffer our separation no longer! she promised herself. It has been too long since I held the orb in my hand. Too long.

However, what she was about to do was risky. She had used magic to accomplish many things, but she had never used it to turn back time.

That's because I have never had my hands on all five of the great powers at once, she reminded herself. The Power of Five is unstoppable! The blonde Guardian used it to restore Caleb – who now lies whimpering at my feet – to life. That is not so far, or different, from my goal. I, too, seek new life!

To reclaim the powers and transform her body, Nerissa would have to use every ounce of magic at her disposal.

To begin with, she would need her four monstrous servants. She had created Ember, Tridart, Khor, and Shagon with the power she had carefully hoarded over her many years of exile. To ensure her success, she would need to borrow some of it back. At best, this would incapacitate her creatures for a time. At worst it would destroy them – and Nerissa would be alone . . . and powerless, once more. That was the one thought that pierced her hardened heart and exposed the dark core of fear that still lay within her. But there was no time for that. It did not pay to be afraid! With courage and confidence, she would bend fate to her will.

She made her way quickly to the captive, who was deep inside among the lava rocks now, close to burning alive. Nerissa called her beasts to gather around him as she began to explain her next move. "An old hag," she proclaimed to them, light flickering across her ruined face. "That's what I have become!" They regarded her stolidly, not daring to respond to their mistress's statements. As the beasts were Nerissa's creations, they knew enough not to question her. Ember, Tridart, Khor, and Shagon just stared into the flames and occasionally looked back and forth between the rogue Guardian and the rebel leader of Meridian.

Nerissa drew a deep breath and spelled out what she would need from her minions. "I only wish to ask a little favor of you," she explained. "But I know I can count on you to help me. I want you to give me back a little bit of the life that I gave to you," she wheedled. "It won't be painful. Not any more than necessary, that is . . ." Lies had always been her stock-in-trade, her standby. There was no reason to speak the truth now. "Believe me," she said with a wicked smile, "this will hurt me much more than it hurts you."

The kindness inherent in those words irritated Nerissa.

They make me sound like the Oracle! She bristled. Weak and too sympathetic. Calling his Congregation to order with false promises. Letting emotions take over.

Nerissa felt the familiar longing to see Candracar again – and to crush it. It would be soon now – *very* soon. She just had to deal with the young Herald first.

She moved towards Caleb, brandishing her staff. "Your hostility is starting to irritate me, Caleb," she said, as she came closer.

Although his body looked spent, his voice still had some fight left in it. "Aren't you tired of failing?" he taunted her. His eyes blazed with anger and determination as he added, "You know I'll never betray Candracar – or its Guardians!"

"If that's the case," Nerissa sneered, "I'll have to get that betrayal out of you . . . against your will!"

She closed her eyes and called to her memory the shame of her sentencing, the pain of her isolation, the years of scheming that had helped her arrive at this moment. She summoned the powers of the elements that screamed all around Mount Thanos: earth and wind, fire and water. She thought longingly of holding the Heart in the palm of her hand once more. She imagined the shining, bright light that awaited her command. Then, when she had gathered all those thoughts together, her empty eyes fixed on Caleb's fearful ones, and Nerissa howled, "May the energy of my creatures sustain me! *I will reclaim the power of the Guardians!*"

With those words, a strong wind rose up, whirling dust and flames into a great tornado. As it spun, the wind gathered strength and speed, mass and sound. *Broooomm!* It sailed past Caleb and ripped him clear from his prison. *Craaaack!* Then it wrapped itself around Nerissa's servants, stripping them of the power she had lent them, leaving them limp and nearly lifeless.

Nerissa surrendered to the power and intensity of the swirling gusts. There was no way to stand up against this awesome power once she had set it in motion – she could only wait to see if it would do her bidding.

For a moment, she felt nothing other than the powerful wind and intense heat. Nothing but the buildup of a mighty power.

Then her body was jolted by a new and electric energy. It was the magic from Khor and his sidekicks, she realised, and it was clicking back into its rightful place. Her heart soared, and her muscles flexed. Her blood raced, and her eyes popped open, ready to regard and embrace the destruction she would unleash. She had all of the strength she needed . . . for now. She was ready to complete the transfer of power.

"May life return, to flow in my veins," she croaked in the stifling atmosphere of Mount Thanos. "Now!"

The volcano strained and groaned. For an instant Nerissa thought that all was lost. Then . . . *kazuuuumm!* it erupted in the one explosion it had been preparing for all its existence, the blast that would shatter it forever – and launch unknown powers back into the world.

Nerissa could not think or focus, but certain sights crossed her line of vision. She saw the body of Caleb launched from the inferno like a rocket, his arms spread out in shock. Then there were her servants, their features twisted in the pain of betrayal. Finally, there was a last gush of lava, spilling out into the frozen tundra all around, coating and melting it beyond recognition. Nerissa watched all the chaos and then threw her head back, overcome with horrible laughter.

She continued to watch the devastation unfold, mesmerized by its beauty and its strength. She could see Khor's hand struggling to gain hold of an outcropping of rock, but she did not deign to help him. It was pointless to bother. Where she was going next, she would not need his help. She no longer – if she had ever – cared what became of any of them. She had used them and would be happy to be rid of them.

As the sounds of chaos grew softer and the air cleared, another strange feeling began to wash over Nerissa. Her body felt lighter, somehow, more flexible and firm. Her vision was keener and her hearing clearer. The bones in her body no longer ached when she bent and twisted. Suddenly, she found that her anger was mixed with a dash of hope, like that of a child.

When she looked at her hands, she couldn't believe what she was seeing. No longer wrinkled or gnarled, they were the hands of a young woman, with clear skin and shining nails. Nerissa was almost afraid to use them, but she slowly lifted one to her head and felt smooth hair where a coarse and tangled mess had been before the explosion. She pulled a handful of it in front of her face, and then she knew for sure. The power had worked! She was transformed! Her hair was as black and glossy as it had been on the day she had gone in chains before the Oracle, humiliated for all eternity. Curls bounced to her waist with the youthful spirit that Nerissa had been certain she would never feel again.

Nerissa jumped to her feet, no longer crippled by the ache of the centuries she had spent inside a tomb. She smoothed her hands over her waist, luxuriating in the fine purple silk that covered her lithe new body, an elegant dress cut low and falling all the way to the ground. She rushed to a pool of melted ice to regard her reflection, and what she saw there brought back so many memories that she staggered backwards for a moment. She remembered them all: Kadma and Halinor, Yan Lin and Cassidy. Especially Cassidy. When I saw her last, I looked like this, Nerissa thought. She felt a pinch of emotion – someone else might have called it regret.

But Nerissa squelched the unwelcome feeling with her usual vigor, and returned to her makeshift mirror, observing her reflection from every angle.

Oh, how the Oracle must have been quaking just then, she thought with satisfaction. The destruction of Mount Thanos would have sent shock waves reverberating through the universe. And surely, deep within Candracar, the Oracle's meditation would have been interrupted. She recalled with a smile that he liked to hover in midair, his legs crossed, in the very centre of his Temple.

Perhaps my act has knocked him to the floor! she thought hopefully. At the very least, it will have opened his eyes. He can no longer be blind to my presence. And soon, he will know the fury of my revenge.

She could just hear his voice in her mind, whispering, "Nerissa, you are lost!" It may have been true back then, she thought gleefully, but it is so much truer now!

"My face . . . my hands . . ." she murmured. "There is a new power within me!" In the clear air of that apocalyptic morning, she collapsed into girlish giggles. And then she announced, to the devastation around her, "Candracar, here I come!"

FOURTEEN

Caleb could hear Nerissa's voice as he crept across the endless ice, every step causing agony to shoot through his body. She was far behind him now, but her words echoed across the vast and frozen tundra. He might have been beyond her sight, but he was not out of earshot yet.

"At last!" he could hear her scream. "How I had tired of this prison of stone! And so, may it disappear forever!"

His ears rang with the *ka-boom!* of disintegrating stone, the continuing roar of lava, and then, another demand from the mistress of Mount Thanos (or what was left of it). "Shagon!" she called. "Where are you?"

He's wherever you sent him, Caleb thought angrily. He didn't exactly like the guy with the snakes for hair, but Nerissa's unjust treatment of Shagon bothered him. She had created him with her own magic, only to sacrifice him for her greater scheme.

It doesn't surprise me, coming from her, but it's not right! Caleb thought. Will he do her bidding now? Where I come from, Shagon would fight back. He would make Nerissa pay for her unfair treatment – like I did with Prince Phobos.

But Shagon was not from Meridian, and he was *not* Caleb. Those rules didn't apply out here. Shagon's eerie voice came floating across the miles, answering Nerissa. "What is your command, Nerissa?" he asked.

"Bring me the captive!" she commanded imperiously. "I don't want to be carrying around any dead weight on our journey."

Caleb shivered, and it wasn't because of the biting wind. But he was on his way to freedom. He looked over his shoulder. First you have to catch me! He thought.

Shagon had to break the bad news to his mistress. "Nerissa!" he said fearfully. "I have news – Caleb has escaped!"

Caleb could only imagine how she would take the news. Nerissa never expected setbacks – and definitely didn't like to admit them, he knew. He could practically see her steely expression, her arms folded across her chest angrily. And then he heard her actual response.

"What a fool!" she shrieked. "Where does he think he's going? Out there he will find only snow and sea . . . and a stinging chill ready to wrap him in a mortal embrace!"

What she said was true, and yet Caleb had one advantage on his side. He had clung to a square of cloth as the explosion set him free. Now it was draped over his head and across his body, providing him some warmth . . . at least for a little while. Against the backdrop of disaster, it was a small triumph. But it meant that he still had a chance to survive.

Still, he was not home free yet. His body was bruised all over from the way he had crash-landed on the ice. His stomach was growling, audible even over the howling of the wind, and he realised that he couldn't remember the last time he'd eaten. Trying not to focus on food, he propelled himself across the wasteland with the positive thought that all was not lost.

I escaped, he told himself. I escaped. But I do not have much time.

He trudged across the snow, with no sense of where he was going except that it was away from Nerissa. He could not pinpoint the length of time he'd been in her clutches, but images of his captivity kept flashing before his eyes. Caleb had seen evil face-to-face before, when he'd served as one of Phobos's Murmurers in Metamoor. Nothing he had seen back then, however, not even the brutal battle to save Meridian, had prepared him for Nerissa's wrath.

I wasn't sure I would make it, he admitted to himself.

He had remained brave while in the belly of the volcano, but he had found no way to get away from the depraved former Guardian until she'd created that powerful wind that had destroyed his cell.

Caleb knew, now, that her revenge was planned down to the smallest detail. He could not help wondering, though, why she had not considered what might happen to him.

Did she assume I would cooperate? he

asked himself. Did she assume I would stay by her side?

Now that he had eluded her, Caleb liked to think that Nerissa wouldn't bother to pursue him. After all, she had claimed his copy of the Guardians' powers, then used the magic to restore herself to her former glory. She had no further use for him that he could think of.

Maybe I have exposed a small flaw in her grand scheme, he thought. Or maybe I have yet to see what she really has in mind for me. He turned his mind from that disturbing thought and plowed on across the ice, a tiny dot in the vast wilderness.

Despite the chill, his thoughts kept going back to his icy prison. He shuddered to remember his last sight of Nerissa, no longer a wizened old woman, but the shining young Guardian she once had been. She was beautiful, really, with her raven-dark hair and her fair skin, her purple dress showing off her slim, strong body. But her beauty was only on the outside. Her soul was full of fury, and her bellowing voice was filled with bitterness . . . and revenge.

It was terrifying to think that the objects of

Nerissa's rage were all that Caleb held dear: his friends, the Guardians. How he wished he could warn them! Caleb thought wearily. They knew Nerissa was after them, eager to seize the Heart, but they had never seen her up close as he now had. They had no idea what kind of power they were up against. And besides, they wouldn't even recognise her in her new form.

Caleb was concerned about his friends. Where were they? He still had faith in their friendship; it didn't seem like the Guardians not to respond. There must be some explanation, he told himself as the many sunrises and sunsets passed in his prison with no sign of Cornelia, his love, or her friends. Something must have happened. He only hoped that they were all safe.

Even as he kept his hope alive, Caleb knew he would have to rely on his own wits to get him through his current situation. There was no prospect of food or water, really, unless he tried to melt some snow in his frozen hands.

If I could only rest, Caleb thought, I could carry on a bit longer. I just need a chance to regain my strength after being in Nerissa's prison for so long. There was nothing in sight, though, except a flat and wintry landscape, and he couldn't very well rest in the open air.

If I don't find shelter soon, it will be the end of me, Caleb realised.

Could he build an igloo with his bare hands? Caleb felt himself grow weaker. He tumbled in the snow. "Ooof!" he cried as he fell to the ground. Instantly, he worried that Nerissa might hear him from Mount Thanos. But then he realised he had a bigger problem. Somebody was standing right in front of him. From where he lay, Caleb could see the bottom edge of a long, red cloak. And as he lifted his gaze, he realised that the cloak belonged to somebody he knew.

Somebody he *didn't* want to see.

Her long hair blew across her face, obscuring it, but her feline profile and frozen whiskers were all too familiar. He thought back on all she had done to hurt him, to separate him from Cornelia. He remembered that, save for her, Nerissa would never have reappeared. But if Caleb could forgive the Guardians, he would have to forgive the Keeper of the Aurameres as well. At the very least, he would have to risk turning to her for help.

Caleb let her see his face, and he threw his arms up in supplication. His mouth was frozen, his lips parched, but somehow he managed to croak, "Please, Luba!"